Little Messenger

Little Messenger

Jayda Lee Wilson

PALMETTO
PUBLISHING
Charleston, SC
www.PalmettoPublishing.com

Copyright © 2024 by Jayda Lee Wilson

All rights reserved

No portion of this book may be reproduced, stored in a retrieval system, or transmitted in any form by any means–electronic, mechanical, photocopy, recording, or other–except for brief quotations in printed reviews, without prior permission of the author.

Paperback ISBN: 979-8-8229-5358-1

Scriptures marked NKJV are taken from the NEW KING JAMES VERSION (NKJV): Scripture taken from the NEW KING JAMES VERSION ®. Copyright© 1982 by Thomas Nelson, Inc. Used by permission. All rights reserved.

Scriptures marked KJV are taken from the KING JAMES VERSION (KJV): KING JAMES VERSION, Public Domain.

Scriptures marked TPT are taken from The Passion Translation ® (TPT), Copyright ©2017, 2018, 2020 by Passion & Fire Ministries, Inc. Used by permission. All rights reserved. ThePassionTranslation.com.

Scriptures marked NASB are taken from the NEW AMERICAN STANDARD BIBLE (NASB): Scripture taken from the NEW AMERICAN STANDARD BIBLE®, Copyright © 2020 By The Lockman Foundation. Used by permission.

Scriptures marked NIV are taken from the NEW INTERNATIONAL VERSION (NIV): Scripture taken from THE HOLY BIBLE, NEW INTERNATIONAL VERSION ®. Copyright© 1973,1978,1984,2011 by Biblica, Inc. Used by permission of Zondervan.

Scriptures marked AMP are taken from the AMPLIFIED BIBLE (AMP): Scripture taken from the AMPLIFIED ® BIBLE, Copyright © 2015 by the Lockman Foundation Used by Permission. (www.Lockman.org)

Scripture marked NLT are taken from the HOLY BIBLE, NEW LIVING TRANSLATION (NLT): Scriptures taken from the HOLY BIBLE, NEW LIVING TRANSLATION, Copyright © 1996,2004,2007,2015 by Tyndale House Foundation. Used by permission of Tyndale House Publishers Inc., Carol Stream, Illinois 60188. All rights reserved. Used by permission.

Scriptures marked TLB are taken from the THE LIVING BIBLE (TLB): Scripture taken from THE LIVING BIBLE Copyright© 1971. Used by permission of Tyndale House Publishers, Inc., Carol Stream, Illinois 60188. All rights reserved. Used by permission.

Scriptures marked NCV are taken from the NEW CENTURY VERSION (NCV): Scripture taken from NEW CENTURY VERSION®. Copyright© 2005 by Thomas Nelson Inc. Used by permission. All rights reserved.

Author Note

It is my pleasure to share God's Word and encouragement through a story. The Holy Spirit once again has shared a brief encounter with me that started through a dream. Once you learn to recognize the leading of the Holy Spirit and are obedient, He will lead you down a path of sixty thousand plus words culminating in a story referencing God's Word. I am amazed once again. I believe God wants us to know that His Word is meant for our lives today, as it was when it was written. Take time to decode what treasures lie within the pages. We all have a purpose in life and if we can use it for Him, then blessings can flow from it and affect this world for the Kingdom. May you find a blessing in this story. You will find that I like to include references to songs with my writing to enhance the message and the experience of the story. At the end of most chapters there will be a song that you can look up and reflect on. I hope that you find this meaningful. It's just another way that God gets His point across to us. I love seeing how He pairs things up so beautifully.

"Now may our Lord Jesus Christ Himself, and our God and Father, who has loved us and given us everlasting consolation and good hope by grace, comfort your hearts and establish you in every good word and work." 2 Thessalonians 2:16,17 (NKJV)

Jayda Lee Wilson

A special thank you to my family and friends for their continued support of my work. I couldn't have made it this far without the patience and encouragement I received from my husband and the added assistance of my dear friend Lori, who always stands ready to read the next book.

Contents

Chapter One: The Report 1

Chapter Two: The Mystery Event 11

Chapter Three: Evil Intent 23

Chapter Four: Danger Revealed 31

Chapter Five: The Warning 47

Chapter Six: Getting Close 59

Chapter Seven: Converging Events 69

Chapter Eight: The Wrong Target 85

Chapter Nine: Answers 95

Chapter Ten: Confidence 105

Chapter Eleven: Angels 113

Chapter Twelve: Twisted Agenda 123

Chapter Thirteen: Morning Chat 137

Chapter Fourteen: Justice 153

Chapter Fifteen: Heaven's Conclusion 167

Chapter Sixteen: Good News 177

Chapter Seventeen: Time of Rejoicing 191

Chapter Eighteen: Reflection 195

About the Author 197

End Notes 198

Chapter One

The Report

Three little girls, all similar in age, were preparing for a birthday party. Guests would be arriving soon; the excitement was growing. There was a flurry of activity going on in the room. An incident had happened earlier in the day that had the adults concerned, but nothing was said out loud.

The President walked into the room, turned and spotted Emily. A big smile rose across his face. Everyone stood up and gave him their full attention. It wasn't just out of respect, it was from the joy they felt being with him, there was an eagerness to run up and greet him from everyone that was around him. He loved children, he saw them as everyone's future and his heart desired what was best for them. He felt this way not only for his children, but for all the children around the nation. As his eyes caught Emily's, he motioned for her to come over to him.

She was very calm and obedient. When she reached him, she wrapped her arms around his waist and gave him a big hug. He leaned over and asked her if she could write a little something about what had happened earlier that day.

She was acknowledging him with a yes, as her eyes looked back at all the buzz going on around the room in preparation for the party.

He noted what was going through her mind and said, "It won't take long. Just a little report on the event." He pats her gently on the back and added, "When you are finished, bring it right to me, no one else."

As she walked past his desk, she grabbed a pad of paper and a pen. She sat down, looked up at all the commotion, then returned her gaze to the blank page and started to write. Tuning out all that was going on in the room she focused on her task. Writing the events of the morning, as she recalled them. Every detail was written down clearly, as if she was writing a book instead of a brief.

The mood in the room changed quickly. The adults looked as if they were concerned about something. The children were asked to gather their things quickly. Emily didn't leave her assignment. The President wanted a report from her, and she was wanting it to be completed.

The First Lady walked up to Emily, encouraging her to finish and gather her things. She didn't use a harsh tone, but it was definitely an urgent tone. Emily was not giving up doing her task at hand.

The First Lady finally grabbed a few of Emily's things, walked over to her with a big smile and told her she could finish that work on the ride, it was time to go.

Struck by the words, 'time to go', Emily spoke up. "The guests are coming for the party. Where are we going?"

Emily's demeanor changed, she was disappointed and confused. She really had not processed what was going on around the room while she was writing her report. It was assumed they were just picking up their things and moving them out of the way for the guests, who would be arriving soon.

"Emily, we have to go, now." The First Lady was encouraging her in a pressed manner.

CHAPTER ONE

Not releasing her hands from the pad and pen, determined not to lose the report she had for the President, she slowly complied. It had become pages long. Everything was detailed. She knew it was important, but she was unaware of just how important, at that time.

She was urged to get in on the passenger side of the car, which was an unusual request. The other two were so distracted by the events of the morning that their focus was on each other and not their surroundings. After Emily slid into the car with the other two girls, the First Lady positioned herself behind the wheel. This was not a typical situation, there was always a driver. Why was she behind the wheel?

As she cranked the car, Emily squealed, "I have to give my report to the President."

"You will, honey." The First Lady softly explained while distracted by what she had to do at that moment. It was important to stay calm.

"No, I have to give it to him, right now." She was unclasping her seatbelt and ready to jump out of the car when the First Lady swung her arm around and grabbed her. "Sit down and buckle up."

The engine roared, the tires spun, and she tore out of the drive as if she was in a racecar and she was destined to be the lead car. The girls leaned back in their seats, bug-eyed. It was apparent now that something big was happening. And the questions remained, where was the driver? Why are we leaving the party?

The car maneuvered through traffic, breaking every speed limit and traffic law there was. The First Lady's eyes were on the road with determination. The girls were in a state of shock at this point. They were unable to ask questions, even though they may have had a whirlwind of them, to share. Things had evolved from a joyous occasion, to one of intense concern.

Once they were out of the fray of town traffic, uncertain where they were headed, Emily finally spoke up and asked the question. "Does this have anything to do with my report?"

After the initial shock had worn off, she was processing the events of the day to what had led up to their apparent escape from something. It seemed to be tied back to her report.

The response from the First Lady was delivered without taking her eyes off the road.

"Honey, I don't know what's in your report, so I can't really answer that question. Do you want to tell me about it?"

"No ma'am, I was told only to share it with the President." She was being respectful yet following instructions from the President.

"I understand, and I don't want you to disrespect his wishes. But you might want to make sure you hold onto that report."

"When will we see the President?"

"I'm not sure, maybe later today. We have a long drive ahead of us."

"Does he know where we are going?"

"Yes, honey. We are all going to the same place. It will be all right."

One of the other little girls was brave enough now, to ask a question. Now that Emily had broken the ice.

"What about the party? What about the guests that were coming?"

"What if I suggest that we have our own special party together." Trying to deflect from the events going on behind them.

"You mean, a private party?" That sounded enticing.

"Yes." She smiled as she was thinking how she was going to pull this one off. She wanted to do something special, but she knew there weren't a lot of provisions where they were going.

The girls were getting tired of riding and needed to make a stop to stretch their legs and get something to eat.

CHAPTER ONE

"Run in, pick up as healthy a snack as you can find, and be mindful of your surroundings."

"Are we in danger?" One of the little girls asked timidly.

"No, of course not, but it's always best to be aware of your surroundings. Now, hurry along."

The first Lady didn't want them doodling out of concern for their safety, as well as she knew she was in a hurry to get to their destination. Emily was a bit slower to get out of the vehicle. She walked over to the First Lady pumping gas.

"I know something is wrong. I feel the danger surrounding us. Is it because of the event this morning? Is it about my report?" She couldn't give up on that train of thought.

At this point, it was hard to hide the truth. "An incident arose at the house, it was thought best that I take you girls to safety, somewhere else. We will be fine, and we will have a celebration." I just don't know how to pull it off, is what she was thinking.

"I was just wondering what happened to our driver?" Emily just couldn't give it up, she knew something wasn't right about the First Lady being the one to drive them.

"We had to move quickly, no time to contact him, that's all." She was hoping that was enough information to satisfy her. But what she was forgetting was that Emily had a photographic memory and was a very gifted child. She didn't miss many details.

Although she was directed to get into the car from the right side, as were the other girls, that should have alerted them to something was awry. Emily picked up on the unusual directives. They were being shielded from the driver's body that lay lifeless outside on the other side of the car. He had been attacked by an assailant, which was a clear indication that their plans had been found out.

The party was going to be used as a diversion for the Presidential family to escape to a secure location away from prying eyes. Once the guest arrived and everyone made an appearance, they were to slip out the rear in separate vehicles. It would have been hard to pull the girls away from the activities and fun, but they were obedient girls and would listen to instructions that were given them. It was always known that being in the presence of power meant being observant, obedient, and to respond quickly.

The First Lady really had not given herself time to think, she had just reacted quickly to the series of events. Now that she sat behind the wheel waiting for the girls to finish up, she took a deep breath and was wondering; had her husband gotten out okay? Was he on the road? Who was with him, and can they be trusted? She was shaken, but she knew she had to hold it together for the girls.

The girls crawled back into their seats, giggling and excited about all their treats.

She could tell they were going to be on a sugar high for a while. Which would lead to a quick crash and silence when they slept it off. The big blue slurpy would likely lead to another stop soon enough, where she would have to fill up the tank, one more time. It was best to always keep a full tank.

It was starting to get late, and the sun was going down. They were almost to their destination. She could breathe a sigh of relief, when she turned on to the dirt drive.

They arrived at a secure mountain cabin, nestled deep in the woods, where there wouldn't be any prying eyes. Drones would not be able to spot the cabin from above, and the trees were so dense that nothing could fly at lower altitudes for surveillance.

There was a huge wraparound porch, where the President was spotted standing on the top steps to greet the girls with a big hug. His wife was amazed

CHAPTER ONE

that he had made it there before she had, but the multiple stops with the girls slowed them down.

After they all had hugs, he stated, "Let's go in, it's getting a bit late to be outside."

As they opened the door, balloons were floating all over the ceiling making it look festive and party-like, there was a birthday cake on the table with dozens of candles that made the cake look like it was on fire. "Surprise!"

The girls squealed with joy. The First Lady squeezed his hand and reached up and kissed him on the cheek. She was relieved, the girls were going to get their celebration after all.

"I don't know how you pulled this off but thank you."

The girls turned to him and said, "But it's your birthday, and you surprised us."

He just smiled and said, "Let's dig in, shall we?"

More squeals of joy filled the room. After things settled down, the girls decided it was time to open presents, then they realized there were no presents. The President and First Lady looked at each other and just smiled back at the girls.

"You are our gift. Nothing more is needed."

Emily spoke up, "But I have a gift for you." She pulled out her report and took it over to him. "You said it was for your eyes only. I've finished it."

He hugged and thanked her. "I know you did a great job. I appreciate all the work you put into this report."

She beamed with pride.

The First Lady stated, "All right girls, it's been one long exciting day and it's time to get some much-needed rest. Wash up and pick the bed that suits you best."

They eagerly rushed upstairs running from room to room, and bed to bed like Goldilocks, trying to pick the best bed. You could hear the giggles flowing through the halls. She shouted after them to be sure to wash their faces before diving into bed. She was exhausted, yet eager to talk with her husband privately.

"I guess you are aware that Tom didn't make it."

"Not until you pulled up without him."

"He was dead, shot in the head from behind. I can only imagine he was taken by surprise." She paused and was confused, then asked, "They didn't inform you of what was going on?"

"Surprising, isn't it? They were doing their job to prevent harm coming towards me, but there was no explanation for what was happening. This was our rendezvous spot, so they brought me here, at my insistence. Of course, I had to make a few stops myself." As he looked around at the celebratory balloons. "Not too much, was it?"

"Perfect." was all she could get out. It was all starting to take a toll on her now, she was reliving the events of the day.

"Is there anything stronger than a soda in this cabin?"

"I had it stocked. Let me fix you something."

He gently touched her arm to demonstrate his concern for her. It had been a traumatic day. Being a woman of great strength and wisdom was a virtue, but a day like today was enough to try anyone's fortitude. It was one thing for them to have made the decision to be in the spotlight, and yes, danger at times, but now with a family, it was harder emotionally on her, putting them in harm's way.

As he was preparing her a drink, she came up behind him and put her arms around him, laid her head on his back and remarked, "I was so worried about you."

"As I was for you all. We will get through this." He was assuring her as he handed her a drink to calm her nerves.

CHAPTER ONE

After a few sips and sitting in silence in front of the fireplace, her curiosity was aroused. Shifting in her seat and looking back at her husband she asked the burning question that she knew he wanted to know about.

"So, what's in that report?"

"Shall we take a look?"

Reaching for the report and smiling at Emily's precise handwriting, he began to read about the events of that morning which Emily incapsulated in her report. They had come to realize that Emily had special gifts that others had not seen. One being her ability to hear from the Lord in special ways, another gift was her attention to detail. The Lord would deliver her messages that were to be shared with the right people, at the right time. Some might even call her a little prophet. When she was younger, caregivers in the orphanage called her touched. Yet, the President and First Lady have come to know her as their daughter, with beautiful gifts.

Emily wrote that an angel appeared at the foot of her bed and delivered a message for the President. Stating that he would be aware that she was given a word for him, and that she was to deliver it at his request. Having written down the Scriptures that were given to her from the angel, she had no explanation of what it meant. The President read them aloud to the First Lady, it was for them to decipher.

"Proverbs 3:13 (NKJV), 'Happy is the man who finds wisdom, and the man who gains understanding.'

Proverbs 3:21-26 (NKJV), 'My son, let them not depart from your eyes---Keep sound wisdom and discretion; So they will be life to your soul and grace to your neck. Then you will walk safely in your way, And your foot will not stumble. When you lie down, you will not be afraid; Yes, you will lie down and your sleep will be sweet. Do not be afraid of sudden terror, Nor of trouble from the wicked when it comes; For the LORD will be your confidence, And will keep your foot from being caught.'

Proverbs 3:31-35 (NKJV), 'Do not envy the oppressor, And choose none of his ways; For the perverse person is an abomination to the LORD, But His secret counsel is with the upright. The curse of the LORD is on the house of the wicked, But He blesses the home of the just. Surely He scorns the scornful, But gives grace to the humble. The wise shall inherit glory, But shame shall be the legacy of fools.'

"Well, that was quite the birthday gift." The First Lady commended him on such a prophetic word.

"Yes, but I will need to unpack all that's there. She has much more here written down about the encounter. I guess that's why it was taking her so long, to get it all outlined. She is such a detailed child." He smiled thinking about how blessed he was to have her as his daughter.

"I believe there was a warning in that Word. If we hadn't been interrupted by the events of the day, she would have given it to you earlier and we may have been able to warn Tom."

"True, but it did say sudden terror. And the Lord would prevent us from being caught up in it. He protected us today and this Word is confirmation of that." He allowed that to sink in.

They watched the flickering of the fire for a while and then he looked in the direction of the bedroom. "I think I'll take the Lord up on some of that sweet sleep. You coming?"

Song "Keep Me In The Moment" by Jeremy Camp

Chapter Two

The Mystery Event

The President was up early the next morning, rereading what Emily had written down. He wanted to process as much as he could before she woke up. If he had questions, he could ask her privately, on a walk around the cabin. There were Secret Service men posted outside guarding them, but they would know to keep their distance during private conversations, although their eyes would never be off the President.

He kept reading what she wrote down. Finding wisdom, does that mean I haven't achieved it yet? Am I to seek better counsel? He pondered those words and then reflected on the part about, "gains understanding."

Thinking out loud to himself. "Does wisdom and understanding not go hand in hand? If I seek counsel from another, I suppose, I need to be able to understand it with a certain amount of clarity. Just as, I'd like to fully understand the meaning of the message from the angel that appeared at the foot of Emily's bed."

She had gone into great detail, describing the angel, what time he had arrived, his tone in which he delivered the message, etc. Was there something he was to gain from all the descriptiveness, or was that just her nature? Thinking this may be a question for Emily to address.

It was true that the girls were a treasure to him, and his wife, they supplied life and a future to their existence. They filled the house with giggles, inquisitive questions, and lots of hugs. They had been unable to have children of their own, and to have the girls be a part of their life was making it more complete. He had used discretion in telling anyone about the gifts Emily possessed. Which is why he had wanted the report delivered only to him. It was for her safety. Emily had delivered other reports to him that had assisted him in decisions which had weighed heavy on his mind. It was part of the reason he ran for office. She seemed to know just what he needed to hear. Specifically, there had been encouragement from the Lord to run for office.

His wife walked in the room, grabbed the coffee pot, and poured him another cup. Realizing that he was trying to dissect the message and was in deep thought.

Placing her hand on his back in a loving gesture, stating with a loving tone, "The message could have simply been a blessing, dear. It was your birthday. After all, it did start with '*Happy is the man who finds wisdom* (Proverbs 3:13 NKJV).' And I know you have wisdom, you selected me to be your bride." She smiled big and kissed him on the cheek.

He swooped her into his lap. "Yes, I did. And I've never regretted it." And he kissed her passionately. The romantic moment was lost when they heard the thud of little feet storming down the stairs. Giggles and squeals were heard throughout the house.

"Ooh, kissing." Was heard from all three.

"Yes, and I have some for you too." As he grabbed the first one that came near, smothering them in kisses on their neck. That's when one of the verses popped back into his head. *"So they will be life to your soul and grace to your neck (Proverbs 3:22 NKJV)."*

Returning to the message, thinking spiritually about the words and trying to define them clearly in his head, he began to break it down. Wisdom is given to the upright that follow God. Wisdom is acting on knowledge provided, and the use of discretion is the capacity of one to analyze and apply the knowledge, in a godly way. So, if I receive information that I am to act upon, I should apply godly methods to achieve the results. For those observing, it will witness to them, whom I follow, and demonstrate to them more of my character.

The perception was the love and care that I show these girls is like the adornment around my neck, witnessing my character through them. How I bring them up will demonstrate the love of Christ. These girls are my adopted children, yet Believers are God's adopted children, and there is no other greater love than the love of God. As he was processing this in his mind, he reached around for another sweet child and hugged and kissed her neck, until he had loved on them all. So thankful to have all three beautiful girls.

"Now what kind of breakfast would you all like? Please, may there be an agreement on one menu, or we will be at the breakfast table until lunchtime." Half-jokingly stated by the master chef when on vacation.

The First Lady was grinning at the sight of her husband as chef and the little helpers he had in the kitchen. She was pleased with the joy that was being shared at this moment, but her thoughts were taking her back to the reality of the day before. There had been plans put in place, as there always was for times of an emergency, but in this case, they had already planned to leave the party early undetected. Who else knew of their plans? As best, she could recall, only Tom knew. It's why he was ready with the car. Is that what gave their plans away? Had it cost Tom his life? She just couldn't shake the sorrow over the circumstances. He was a good man, a confidant and reliable person, someone she and the girls trusted.

The First Family enjoyed escaping to the cabin in the woods, or to a remote beach somewhere for privacy and relaxation. It was good for the girls to have one-on-one with them and not be surrounded by aids and bodyguards all the time. They just needed time to be a family. The getaway had been planned as his birthday gift, and the party had been designed to be the perfect diversion. The girls only understood that they were celebrating the President's birthday, and there were going to be lots of guests coming. But the events of that early morning had stirred concern, as to whether they should rethink their plans, or cancel them altogether.

It was still not known if there was a real threat that happened that night, or not. Nothing was revealed from the search. When these types of things occur, they are instructed to be silent about them, so as not to cause a reaction in the media, where things can be blown out of proportion, creating more of a problem. But apparently something had taken place. Tom had died. Secret Service had spotted a body down, and it set things in motion for the escape.

When the angel appeared at Emily's bed, she was not frightened. This happens frequently as a seer, one who can see the supernatural. Angels were one of the ways in which the Lord spoke to her. It was a call on her life, her assignment to deliver messages. Her encounters with angels started when she was young, possibly before she was placed in the system. At first, the angels appeared to her as a comfort, a means to watch over her. As she aged, they gave her guidance from God. They were giving her specific instructions to share messages with others. Messages of encouragement, strength, guidance and at times warnings. This seemed odd from one so young, therefore she was not taken seriously until she was united with her new parents.

The night before, as a special treat in preparation for the celebration, the girls were allowed to sleep together in the same room. Emily had the king-sized bed, so they selected her room to bunk in. June was aroused from sleep and was

CHAPTER TWO

startled by something, she screamed bloody murder. When one screams, they all scream. This set off a series of commotion in the entire house.

All emergency lights came on. Secret Service were swarming the premises, going through every room, every closet, and searching the grounds. Lights were on, as if it were daylight out. The President and First Lady could not get to the girls, because the incident was perceived as a threat taking place, so they were in lockdown. The girls were upset by all the people in their room and the chaos that seemed to ensue. They remained silent, afraid to speak. Not a peep was heard from the initial screams.

Emily knew what she had seen, but she was surprised that June saw the same thing. Emily wasn't saying a word, so June followed her example. Emily knew that most people wouldn't understand, even if she tried to explain, so it was best to remain quiet and share with only people who were willing to listen with open minds, that was her parents who were being kept from them until things were resolved.

It was puzzling to her that June was able to see the angel too. At least, that was what she was assuming at that moment. Normally no one else was able to see or hear her angel. Could she have seen something or someone else in the room? She wouldn't know until she had an opportunity to talk with June privately, to know for sure what made her scream. It remained a mystery.

The morning carried on at the cabin; breakfast was finished up, followed by a lot of rubbing of the tummies, stating how full they were. They had enjoyed a huge stack of pancakes with crispy bacon, just the way they liked it. They had created a huge mess, and they knew it was theirs to clean up.

The First Lady needed answers as to what had happened to Tom. She was eager to speak to her husband alone, so she encouraged the girls to play on the porch outside. There were no complaints from the girls about leaving the dishes in the sink. She pulled her husband aside and shared that she just couldn't shake what had happened the day before, the concern was still heavy on her heart. As they cleaned up after the girls, they were able to discuss things out of the earshot of the three that knew nothing of Tom's death.

Now free to share what was on her mind, it came spilling out uncontrollably. "Was the event during the night connected to Tom's death? We know that Emily had a visitation because she had a report to give you. Was the commotion at night only about the angel? Or was the angel warning us, putting us all on high alert? Should we even be out here, in the wilderness, away from all the security? It's not just about us anymore, we must consider the safety of the girls."

"I'm having the same kinds of questions, honey. But I do believe we are safe here, no one knows where we are. We have security who has surrounded us up here. You just don't see them because their job is to remain out of sight."

"Do you think they were after you, or could they have been after the girls?" She couldn't shake the feeling of trouble ahead.

"That's the question that needs to be answered. Ultimately, if it were the girls, then they were wanting something from me. Some sort of ransom, for another outcome."

"What else was in the report from Emily? Didn't you say there was more?"

"Oh, she just went into great detail about the angels."

"Angels? That's plural. How many were there? Why more than the messenger?"

"I don't know the answer to why, but the how many, was three."

"Three, was it the girl's guardian angels? Were they there to protect them?" Fear for the girls started to surface.

"Again, I don't know the reason for multiple angels. But everyone has a guardian angel and some people have more than one. They could have all been there for Emily. She was the one who was supplying us with a report from them."

"True, but as a seer, she could have seen the girl's angels." Pausing, then asking,

"Did they all deliver a message to her?"

"No, apparently there was only one that was speaking."

"What else was said? You're leaving something out."

"I believe the commotion disrupted the full message. But she did quote more of *Proverbs 4:20-23(NKJV)* which warns about the condition of the heart."

"Well, what exactly does it say? It must be important for it to have been a message to be delivered to you. Or do you think it was a message for Emily?"

He was pulling out the report that he was carrying around with him, for security reasons, his eyes only, was the way he looked at it. He also wanted it close so that he could look back over it, hoping to determine its full meaning.

"It reads, *'My son, give attention to my words; Incline your ear to my sayings. Do not let them depart from your eyes; Keep them in the midst of your heart; For they are life to those who find them. And health to all their flesh. Keep your heart with all diligence, For out of it spring the issues of life.'*"

"Well, I'd say it's telling you to get your heart in the right place. Is there something you need to tell me?"

He smiled at her and shook his head. "You know everything about me, including where my heart lies."

He grabbed her hand and gave it a squeeze. "I believe it's telling me to prioritize His Word and listen carefully to instructions and obey them. Our actions reflect our hearts, and we need to guard against bad counsel. It could be a life and death situation we are to be vigilant about. I may want to more closely vet the people I bring into my inner circle." Shaking his head. "I'm still working on it."

"Well, those verses mention ears, eyes, and heart, things we open ourselves up to. I imagine you are to be careful what you see and hear, because it will affect your heart. Don't always rely on your senses, rely on what's in your heart. Avoid making irrational decisions based only on what you see."

"You my dear, are a wise woman."

"Yes, I'm glad you recognize that." She smiled big and continued with, "I may be misusing these words to my benefit, but I believe Proverbs 4:5 (NKJV) says something like, *'Get Wisdom! Get understanding! Do not forget, nor turn away from the words of my mouth. Do not forsake her, and she will preserve you; Love her, and she will keep you. Wisdom is the principal thing; Therefore, get wisdom. And in all your getting, get understanding. Exalt her, and she will promote you; She will bring you honor, when you embrace her.'"*

"You quoted well. Now, allow me to embrace you."

He grabbed her by the waist and pulled her into himself and kissed her passionately. It was not something they were able to extend towards one another in the public eye, so these were their special moments to demonstrate how much they were still in love with each other.

The office of the President is very demanding and leaves very little private time. Quiet get-aways are important to them, as a couple, and as a new family. They depended on each other for advice and a good measure of grounding themselves. They didn't want being in the public eye to affect them as a couple, nor for it to influence the girls in any negative way. They wanted to capture special moments together.

They were so happy to have made the decision to adopt the girls, completing their family. Joy filled their home, all in a new way. They had tried to have children for years and were unable to fulfill that dream, until God gave them another dream, an instant family. Adoption proceedings had started long before the decision to run for office. These proceedings always took longer than one would expect, even if you had money and influence on your side.

The Patterson's had traveled the world through business dealings prior to getting into politics. They had seen the world and made many connections around the globe, but it was time to settle down and get focused on a family. At that point in time is when their attention was drawn to the condition of society, and how it would affect their children's future. They felt that they could make a difference, bringing their expertise to the nation. Opening the eyes of the people to solutions found in other nations, applying good business practices, and bringing ideas of ways to improve foreign trade. It was always thought that their lives should reflect their goals that they wanted to achieve. Their new goal was to blaze a foreseeable path for the next generation. But they wouldn't give up on the dream of a family for themselves.

Emily had been the first child they adopted, which took place two years before they entered the race for President. Emily had a special assignment given to her at birth, and her angel was there to prepare her for this special work. The Patterson's had not been told of her gifts because they were misunderstood, it was thought that she was mentally unstable and would need special care. This kind of labeling had made it difficult to place her in any home. Emily had been in the system since she was about two years old. There had been little information about her past. The Patterson's had the funds to accommodate a special needs child, and felt it was their calling to take a child that had been hard to place. When they were introduced to her, they only saw a beautiful child needing a home and someone to love her.

Emily had learned to be obedient and advised to keep to herself. This had helped her to stay out of trouble and free from discipline. Although there had been many years of being shuffled from one facility to the next, throughout the system. It was felt that if she had been extra good, she could stay in one place and establish some semblance of home. She had no idea that she was about to be placed in the perfect home.

Emily's angel had assured her that they were going to be loving parents and could be trusted with her gifts. That she was going to be asked to open-up to them and share what she was being told. Her new father was one she needed to deliver messages to. This had been a shock to her new parents at first, but they listened and were not judgmental. With time, they found that she had been correct about what had been delivered through her messages. Trust had been established.

It wasn't long after Emily had come to live with them that she had a message about siblings. At first, it was thought, she was missing all the children in the orphanage, so they lavished more gifts and love on her, to occupy her mind. Then she received a specific message about two girls, siblings, and they would be coming to live with them to complete their family. This came as a surprise, thinking they had completed their family with Emily, but they liked the idea of a full house. They had quizzed her more about what she had heard.

Emily informed them that it was twin sisters that had been hard to place, because they refused to be separated. This news broke her mother's heart. Why would anyone want to separate siblings? Clearly her family was about to expand without any preparations.

The words came flooding from her heart. "Who would want to separate siblings, of course they want to be together, it's known how emotionally attached twins are to each other."

Without even discussing it fully with her husband she immediately stated, "How do we find them?"

He knew the heart of his wife and once her mind was made up, there was no turning around. She would search every facility, from here to around the world, until she found them. It kind of reminded him of Jesus, searching out the lost sheep. How He would leave the flock to look for the lost one in Luke 15:5,6 (NKJV). *"And when he has found it, he lays it on his shoulders rejoicing. And when he comes home, he calls together his friends and neighbors, saying to them 'Rejoice with me, for I have found my sheep which was lost!"*

CHAPTER TWO

He had told her that he would scour the system for them. There had been many sleepless nights, until they got word of twin girls that refused to be separated.

"It has to be them." She shouted.

June and April were soon under the same roof with them. The family was complete. Love and laugher filled their home. Emily, although similar in age, was still seen as the older, wiser sister, because she had come to the family first and demonstrated more maturity.

June and April were not identical twins, but they were inseparable. They were both talented young girls. June, an auburn-haired beauty, was a quiet child comforted by music. She had a special ear and talent for music, her passion was the violin. At the age of ten, she already knew she wanted to be a composer when she grew up. The house was filled with her original tunes.

April, fair skinned and blonde, was creative and flamboyant with artistic abilities. Her character and emotions were on display through her art, with the use of bright and aggressive colors. The President's office was filled with her inspired masterpieces.

God had orchestrated a masterpiece in bringing this family together.

Song "Always" by Chris Tomlin

Chapter Three

Evil Intent

The girls were pleased to be alone with their parents on what they saw as an excursion. Happy to have celebrated their father's birthday, even if it was a private party, the ones that counted were present. It was funny how well the girls got along and how much they had in common. They were not only sisters, but they were best friends, true companions. They had jumped rope for a while outside, until they decided it was time to swing in the hammock. They were all rolled up as one, pulling on the rope over them, designed to give them momentum for a higher swing. The giggles filled the porch.

Emily got still for a moment. She was sensing something out of the ordinary. They were always being watched, but this felt different, it felt as if there were some sort of evil intent.

Without explanation she stopped pulling the rope and suggested to the other girls, "I think it's time to go in."

"Not yet, we are enjoying the swing." June exclaimed.

"Pull harder," came from April, "Don't stop."

"No, it's time to go in," she stated emphatically.

June and April were both disappointed, they wanted to swing longer, but they knew that Emily was just watching out for them. Even though they were close in age, the twins looked up to Emily. She was more mature and wiser beyond her years, even the girls could sense that. Once inside, Emily didn't make a big deal of it, but she slid the lock in place and went and sat down.

"I think it would be a good time to read until Dad gets back." She was wondering where her parents had gotten off to.

She followed up with, "Maybe he will play some games with us."

Looking around for a deck of cards or something to set up for when he came back in, she was trying to shake the feeling that she was having. Telling herself that it must have something to do with the other night's commotion. But she had experienced the same feeling when they had stopped for gas, on the way up here. She didn't always understand the messages she delivered to people, but she did recall that this message had something about sudden terror and trouble from the wicked, in it. It was a warning of some sort. Maybe it was time to have a conversation with June about what she saw that night.

She turned to look at June and noticed that April had decided to nap instead of reading. This may be a good time to talk to her about what made her scream. She asked June to come sit next to her. June laid her book down and moved over to the sofa where Emily was sitting.

"What's up?"

"You've stayed silent about the events of the other night. Can I ask, what scared you?"

Shivering as if she was reliving it, she replied to Emily. "I saw someone."

"Or something?"

"No, someone." She was emphatic about what she saw.

"Where? In the room?" Seeking more details.

"No, on the balcony."

"June, we have people on the balcony to protect us."

"No, it was someone trying to come through the window."

"What!" Now Emily was shocked.

"I thought you saw him too." June stated confused.

"No, I didn't see anyone trying to come in the window. Why didn't you say something about it earlier."

"You, didn't say anything, so I was afraid to say anything."

"Oh my, I think we should have had this conversation before now. We need to tell Mom and Dad as soon as possible."

"Where are they, anyway?"

"I think you call it, alone time."

"Well, I think we need some together time."

"Me too." The girls got up from the sofa and started down the hall to their parent's room, calling out for them.

The door opened and with concerned faces, the parents questioned the girls. "What's wrong, is everyone all right?"

"Yes, we are fine, but I think we should talk. Maybe you and I could share a minute alone and then we could all be together." Emily needed to give them an overview of what she had just been told, and June didn't need to hear what she was to share.

June piped in, "Some together time, please."

"Sure thing, where is April?" Counting heads and only coming up with two.

"Napping in the den."

"Well, let's go collect her and see if we can rustle up some lunch." The First Lady was aware that Emily was wanting some one-on-one time. As a mom, she had developed a sense of what the girls were always needing.

Closing the door behind him, he took a seat on the bed, waiting for Emily to unload her concerns. "What's on your mind, sweetie?"

Not sure where to begin yet snuggling up close to her father as a comfort, she started to explain how she got a weird feeling at the gas station and then again, a little while ago.

"Okay, that's understandable concerning the events that have taken place."

"Well, that's not all." She paused trying to fit it all in.

She was a detailed person and she wanted him to get the whole picture. Sometimes it's crucial as to which piece of the puzzle you put into place first, in order to help discover what's next. By starting out with how she was getting an uncomfortable vibe was letting him know that there was something to be concerned about.

"I think the angels were warning us of some type of danger. It may be why there was more than one angel this time."

He was giving her his full attention, listening carefully to her every word because he had questions about that as well.

She continued. "The message for you was about a sudden terror and trouble from the wicked. Maybe that was for us. Someone tried to come through the window that night."

His eyes got wide in shock and his mouth dropped open as if he wanted to say something, but nothing came out. He simply reached across to Emily and drew her close, knowing this is what she needed most at that moment, to be secure in his arms. Revealing this kind of information had her shaken. It had all become real. She was feeling the danger.

"You're okay, it's all going to be okay." He was comforting her.

"I've never tried to unravel the messages, I just deliver them, but this one seems different. Maybe it was intended for me." Sounding a little scared.

"Let's go back to the man coming through the window. Why haven't you said something about this before now?"

"I didn't see him; it was June who saw him. I thought she saw the angels. I just thought she was staying quiet about it because she didn't know how to describe them. I asked her about it just a few minutes ago, and that's why I wanted to talk to you privately about it."

"You're right, you did the right thing, honey." Thinking how wise she was for her age.

He was holding her and rocking her in his arms while processing for himself what to do next. She had no idea about Tom being killed. They were assuming that her eerie feeling at the gas station was regarding his murder beside the car. But now, she was having that feeling outside on the porch. Was it something she couldn't shake, or was it something else that they needed to be concerned with? Was it a warning?

"Let's not worry the others, shall we. You go on in the kitchen and help with lunch. I'll be right behind you."

She gave him a big hug and tried to put on a smile for the others. But she couldn't get rid of the feeling of danger looming around her. As soon as she was out of the room, he turned and pulled out his revolver and checked it to make sure it was loaded.

He was now concerned about the men he brought up here to protect them. Could it be one of them that they should be afraid of? He wasn't taking any chances; he would continue to carry protection for himself, to keep his family safe. He had been in the military and knew how to handle a gun proficiently. The time had come that they may need to make some other arrangements. He needed to talk with his wife.

Reciting part of the message in his head looking for guidance. "*For the LORD will be your confidence And will keep your foot from being caught (Proverbs 3:26, NASB).*"

"Well Lord, help us in our time of need." He whispered.

As he entered the kitchen, he checked the lock on the door, and gazed outside trying to spot the men that were keeping watch over the cabin.

Contemplating that they wouldn't try anything in broad daylight. Nightfall comes early in these parts; decisions needed to be made quickly.

He broke the silence by growling like a bear. "I'm so hungry, I could eat a horse. But I don't see a horse, I see three little tasty girls."

He came up behind each one tickling them as if he was going to eat them. Giggles broke out including from the First Lady. She loved watching the demonstration of love he had for the girls.

They enjoyed lunch together and then he insisted that they play some family games together in the den. June and April were wanting to go back outside and swing. Emily was hesitant to say anything, but it was detected that she didn't want to go outside.

"No, no, this is our together time, remember. We are going to have a great time right here in front of this big fireplace."

The First Lady knew something was up, so she played along. She knew he would explain when he got a chance. The fireplace was warm and inviting, giving them comfort, and game time ensued with jokes, followed by laughter.

The danger lurked nearby, outside the cabin. The man that tried to get into the girl's room was the same man that was concealed under the leaves, beyond the car. He had missed his opportunity on the balcony at the mansion. Needing access to wherever they were headed, he figured no better location than to hitch a ride in the same vehicle. He had walked over Tom's lifeless body and entered the trunk of their car.

Once they arrived at the cabin and a deep darkness enveloped the grounds, he was able to slip out of the trunk and hide among the leaves. Positioning himself close enough to the house to make his next move. As he lay there, he was making a mental note of the routine of the Secret Service, hoping to move in when they were at the furthest position from the house. Their eyes had mostly been on the surrounding areas of the cabin and the movements of the

CHAPTER THREE

President, not the vehicles. He had been so close to the girls when they were outside jumping rope, but so were the Secret Service. It had not been the right time to make his move.

The President decided he needed to stretch his legs, sitting Indian style was not the most comfortable position for a man of his age. He got up and walked in the direction of the bedroom while eyeing his wife, giving her the signal to follow him.

She made her excuse to run to the bathroom, giggling like she had held it too long, which made the girls laugh. The girls also got up to stretch and to fetch some snacks, filling up on some of the leftover birthday cake. When the First Lady made it to the bathroom, he gently closed the door behind her.

"Now, I know you are not trying to flirt with me. What's going on?"

"We have a dangerous situation on our hands." Until now, he had tried to withhold this information, but it was time to share his concerns with his wife without her panicking.

"What?" She looked stunned. "How bad?"

"I'm focusing on the fact that God is on our side." Trying to find a positive in their situation.

"Well, now, I'm really worried. You're calling in the big guns."

"Speaking of guns, I am carrying." Her eyes got big, and he continued, "I have to protect you all, the best way I can."

He proceeded to share what Emily had unloaded on him earlier. Adding, "I'm not sure if this is friendly fire or if there is another source to our situation. But we have to be observant to every detail."

"Friendly fire?" That didn't slip by her unnoticed.

"We can't be too sure about anything, or anyone. Our own protection could be our biggest threat. There are too many pieces of the puzzle missing."

"Kind of reminds me of our conversation this morning. The one about being vigilant, staying on guard."

"Yes, it's funny how that fit into our day."

"What's your plan?"

"At first, I thought it would be good to just board things up and stay put, but the more I thought about that, it didn't make sense to hunker down here. We'd be sitting ducks. It will be dangerous, but I think we should try and make a run for it."

"A run for it? We don't even know who we are running from. And where to?"

"I realize that's what makes this even more dangerous."

"Go on, what's the plan." She was listening intently.

"I think they will make a move when it gets dark. That gives them cover, as well as us. So, we need to be ready to move fast when the sun sets. The darkness will shield us to a degree, but surprise and speed will be the most important element. Don't worry about belongings, we will just dart to the car and leave before anyone can react. It will be unexpected from us and that is to our advantage."

Song "Raise A Hallelujah" by Jonathan Helser

Chapter Four

Danger Revealed

The man from the trunk of the car had made his way up to the porch, shielding himself next to the air conditioner, to keep from being sighted by the family and the secret service. Hearing voices coming from a cracked window in the bathroom, he leaned in, overhearing the parents' plan to escape. For the family to remain within his grasp, he would have to hitch a ride in the trunk again. Not the best accommodations, but it was his only mode of transportation. He would have to time his actions precisely, or it could be deadly for him.

The President was explaining to the girls, in as simple terms as possible, the plans to leave the cabin they were in to find another location to have family time. He didn't want to scare the girls, but at some point, it was going to be clear that they were running from someone. The girls were collecting their things when he mentioned no electronic devices. This raised some moans from the girls. His wife understood that devices meant tracking. That's when she looked in his direction and asked the question that couldn't be fully answered.

"But what about the car? Isn't it wired with some sort of monitoring system?"

A system that was designed to protect them is now considered part of the problem. There was no time to layout his plans further and there certainly wasn't another alternative. He was patting himself down and realized he didn't have the keys.

"You have the keys?" He asked, not wanting to get to the car empty handed.

"Yes."

"It's getting dark." It was what they were waiting on.

He paused and was looking around outside to see where the security detail was located. No one was close enough to the cabin or the cars, to be detected. He looked back at his wife and said with an urgent voice, "It's time."

The girls were huddled near the door with their mom, waiting for the sign to go. They had been instructed not to dally, but to go straight to the car as fast as they could. Hearts pounding and fear mounting, they all darted out to the car. He got behind the wheel, revving up the engine and threw it into reverse, spinning the car around. When shots were fired.

Were they trying to stop an attacker, or were they trying to stop the vehicle? The shots were useless towards this car, the tires couldn't be shot out, because they were protective tires, and the windows were bulletproof. One thing was proven, the threat had been real.

Everyone was silent.

They proceeded down the dirt road as fast as he could manage the car and out onto the blacktop, where he could get real speed. He needed the head start or it was going to be a dangerous chase, which could end in a disastrous result.

The Secret Service pursued them, as it was their job to do. The fleeing from the cabin had caught them off guard. They were now looking at each other, trying to figure out who fired the first shots, not sure who to trust given their

CHAPTER FOUR

present circumstances. One thing for sure, there must be a credible threat with all that was going on. They had been made aware of the driver's body being found in DC, but they believed that they were separated from the danger out here in the woods. Why were shots being fired at the vehicle? Had one of the agents thought someone else was trying to drive away? Why was the President and his family fleeing?

They had been driving for a short time, the girls remained quiet in the back seat. It was now very clear that they were under attack and were being chased, this was no typical change of venue for family time.

The President was thinking out loud, "We need to get rid of this car."

He glanced in his wife's direction and said, "If you spot a car without a driver whether it's in a driveway or a parking lot, let me know. We are going to have to ditch this car and borrow another."

This was the answer to getting rid of the car with the monitoring system. He feared that the Secret Service would have called in the incident by now and would detect their location soon. He wasn't sure how they would have reported the events that occurred, as to not get themselves tied to any backlash. The important thing was to disappear.

It was less than a minute later when she shouted, "I see one, in the drive to your right."

"Okay, I'm going to pull up and hotwire it, and you are going to drive this vehicle about five miles or so down the road, I'll follow. Look for a dirt road to pull down before you stop. We'll ditch this car and you and the girls join me in our new ride."

"Good plan, dear."

She was so proud of her husband. He was quick to make decisions and he was courageous, not faltering in protecting them. In her mind he stood ten feet tall and was capable of anything, even hotwiring a car. Now that was something she'd have to ask him about later.

"I'm going to call Allen, to see who he thinks we should reach out to for protection."

"We don't have our phones."

"No, but we will have to stop for gas at some point, and I will ask to use someone else's phone to call."

"Won't you be recognized?"

"Without an escort I kind of doubt it."

"Won't they be able to trace the call to the location of the gas station and know our direction?"

"Yes, they will do that, but I think we will be down the road by the time they trace a call and send someone in this direction. We will be long gone."

"Okay, but how do we know we can trust Allen?"

"At some point, I have to trust someone. He is my Vice President, the one that brought us into all of this mess. I feel he should help us get out of this pickle we are in."

He was shaking his head. "I don't know if it's the right thing to do, but I do know that we need help. We will need some security, and we can't remain on the run forever. He is a long-time friend, and he knows the political system, surely, he has connections with security details, someone he trusts."

Jim Patterson was the man with stellar character, charisma, intelligence, and a smile that lit up a room and warmed people's hearts. A man that the public admires and trust. He was talked into running for President by Allen Crandall, his college buddy, who had been in politics for years. He knew the ropes and was able to convince Jim that the nation needed him. Jim had always been successful at whatever his endeavors were, so he thought, why not. He has run corporations, why not a nation. At first it was a joke, between two college buddies, until it became their reality.

They made the car exchange. The hotwiring came easy, something he had done in his younger days, that he wasn't particularly proud of, yet was proving

CHAPTER FOUR

to be an advantageous skill at the moment. He would have to explain that to the girls later. It had taken more like eight miles before they came to a dirt road to pull onto. Jim directed them to drive the limo further down the dirt road, as not to be seen by the traffic from the main road. He knew the secret service would find it sooner or later through the monitoring system, but this gave them some time to change course and try to throw their assailant off a bit more, whoever it was that tried to shoot them.

They were unaware of the extra passenger in the trunk. Although it was hard to follow their full conversation, he did manage to pick up on the words, Vice President. That gave him a clue as to how to find them. Things had not gone as he planned, but he had managed to stay with the family up to this point, and he was happy about the breadcrumbs being left behind, for him to follow.

After the car left with the First Family, he hopped out of the trunk and slipped behind the wheel to drive a ways down the road, until he found another ride. Understanding the reason why they ditched the overly surveilled car. He too didn't want to be tracked and found in their vehicle.

Settling into the drive, in their newly acquired vehicle, Jim looked into the rearview mirror and noticed the other two girls were sound asleep, yet Emily was staring out the window taking in the scene of a beautiful night sky, or pondering what has happened.

He turned his head toward Emily and whispered, "I know you have connections with angels, it would be a good time to ask them for advice."

Emily responded, "We all have connections with angels, Dad." She paused a minute and added, "I asked once, why I could see them, and others couldn't. My angel said it was because I believed in them and the supernatural. Others have too much unbelief which blocks their ability to see. And Dad, it doesn't work that way, they come to me with messages, I just deliver what I'm asked to."

"Well, we are needing one of those messages. I believe in you. Feel free to deliver advice at any time."

She felt the pressure now, as if it was her responsibility to get them out of the trouble, they were in. She had never called on the angels before, they just appeared at her bedside, when God asked them to deliver a message. She'd never thought about asking them for some specific help before. However, she knew they were always watching over her.

Gas was needed to stay on the road. The stop would give him an opportunity to call Allen. At this point he was just headed north, not sure where he was going, but knew that when daybreak came the girls would need to eat and stretch their legs. Accommodations would eventually need to be made. Maybe Allen would have some ideas for a safe haven. He also thought that a swap in vehicles would be needed again. The owners may have reported it stolen by now and drones would be out soon. He hoped that no one would recognize him when he stopped. It was common knowledge that credit cards could be traced, so he would have to use cash, which will run out fast enough with gas and food.

"Allen, I'm glad you picked up. I'm in a pickle."

"I'd say so, it's all over the news. I don't know how they got it out so quickly. It will be hard to remain unnoticed. Who are you running from?"

At this point Allen was unaware that they were on the run once again. He was referring to the incident at the mansion.

"I'm not really sure. I know there is a threat, because of Tom's death. But I am suspicious of our surveillance team."

"What? You mean one of your own agents?"

"Yes, shots were fired at the cabin. And there is more, but I don't have time to go into it right now. I need to know that you have my back." There was silence on the other end. "Can you arrange help? Allen are you there?"

"You know I have your back. I'm just processing what you're needing. I'm two steps ahead of you. Where are you?" He sounded very reassuring, which brought Jim comfort.

Jim proceeded to give him the direction he was headed in, and asked about a secure site to hideout, until another security detail could assist them.

It only took moments for Allen to respond with a safe house in that area. He gave Jim the directions to the house and followed up with scripture to encourage him and remind him, that he was always successful. It was one of the things that Allen admired about Jim, he always worked things out where he was on top.

What Allen failed to witness was that it required a lot of work and faith to make it happen. There had been plenty of times where Jim felt things were going to blow up in his face, but he didn't give in, and he never gave up. Jim had always been reminded of the verse in Galatians 6:9 (NKJV), *"And let us not grow weary while doing good, for in due season we shall reap if we do not lose heart."* It was a message of persistence, and to know that things will be fulfilled and work out in God's time. Never underestimate God, and trust in the calling that he has on your life, is advice Jim would give to Allen.

The verse that Allen spoke over Jim, in his time of need was Joshua 1:8-9 (NCV), *"Always remember what is written in the Book of the Teachings. Study it day and night to be sure to obey everything that is written there. If you do this, you will be wise and successful in everything. Remember that I commanded you to be strong and brave. Don't be afraid, because the LORD your God will be with you everywhere you go.'"*

"Don't worry Jim, I've got your back, things will work out."

Jim appreciated the words of encouragement from a good friend that had his back, he needed to be reminded to be strong and brave and that the Lord was with them.

They were able to find the house, after they had found the drive-through for breakfast. The girls were pleased to be fed, and Jim was aware that his funds were depleting faster than anticipated. Cash is all one should use on the run. The girls got out of the car and were glad they could stretch out after being cramped up in the back seat of the much smaller car for hours.

The First Lady remarked, "Well, this certainly is remote enough. How did Allen know about this place?"

"He has had his hands in all kinds of positions in politics, I'm sure he has come across safehouses as well."

"Jack of all trades." She smiled.

"Yes, he really came through for us, in a pinch. I believe he is working on a new security detail as well. After telling him about our concern with the last detail, I'm sure he will vet this group thoroughly."

"For now, let's focus on the girls and their needs. I know they must be scared."

"That's what I love about you, it's always about someone else's needs. How are you holding up?" He reached over to give her a little hug.

She smiled and shrugged her shoulders, trying to hold it all together. She knew if she gave in to her fears she would fall apart, she was worried about the girls. He could see that in her eyes, and he wasn't going to push her over the edge. She was demonstrating her strength and courage; he was very proud of her.

"I'll be fine. But the shots fired did unnerve me. I just don't understand what's going on. Why do they want the girls?"

"I'm sure it's for leverage. Someone wants me to do something for them. I just don't know which group would be involved in kidnapping. And how did they get the Secret Service involved? Or did they? Could we be wrong? Has someone else found us? Could we have been running from our help?"

CHAPTER FOUR

"Don't second guess yourself now. Let's just deal with what we have at hand."

They let the girls run around outside for a little while, thinking no one could have followed them up here, as remote as this place was. April found a beautiful bird feather. She was showing it to the other girls when Emily told her, "That is a sign that your guardian angel is near."

"What do you mean? Isn't this just a bird feather?" She was confused. Pondering the thought of angels being that small.

"Yes, but it's a sign." Emily was trying to frame the explanation.

"A sign?"

"It could be a message, a direction or guidance that will be revealed, but a sure sign that your guardian angel is nearby. A sign that we aren't alone."

"I know we aren't alone; mom and dad are here with us."

"You're right April. It's a beautiful feather."

She knew April didn't understand, and there was little point in explaining it all, right now. But she had been told that finding a feather could have various meanings, that one would be healed from an illness or a sign of good news coming. It could also be a spiritual meaning of hope and comfort during a time of disappointment. Which they were surely a part of right now.

The angels had shared lots of little tidbits of knowledge with Emily over the years. She had learned to treasure their visits and kept them to herself. When she had tried to share encounters with others, they labeled her, and it became a detriment to placing her in a home. She had been in the system since she was two years old. Now she was able to reflect on what had happened and realized she was just waiting on the perfect home.

As the sun was setting, they decided it was best to take refuge inside. Within a few hours; they heard a car pulling up outside. Jim went to the window to check things out and recognized it was secret service carrying a badge and a bag full of groceries.

There was a knock at the door. Jim pulled his revolver out just in case.

"Who sent you?"

"Allen."

"We appreciate the groceries; you can leave them at the door, and we will get them.

Hope you can understand that no one is coming near my girls."

"Understood. We are here to help, not cause more trauma to the girls."

"I appreciate your understanding."

They placed the groceries down and backed away from the door. The agent continued down the steps explaining, "They would keep their distance and keep an eye on the perimeter. When they get word from Allen that the coast is clear, to move back to Washington, he would notify them. If they needed anything, they could use the disposable phone in the bag."

Jim was relieved that Allen had thought of everything. It was good to have such a friend as close as Allen in the depths of DC. He had shown him the ropes of the political realm and had fought beside him to get his agenda done for the people. Now, he was coming to his aid, to help his family out of a very tight spot. He would owe Allen big.

When things settled down a little, Jim was able to reflect on what Emily had said about the angels. She hadn't ever called on them, they came to her with messages to share with others. He guessed that made sense, we are to call on Jesus, not angels, Jesus is our Lord and Savior. Jesus sends the angels to our aid. He was now wishing he had asked Emily more about her encounters with angels. Who all she had given messages to over the years? What kind of messages did she deliver?

Having done some research on angels when he found out about Emily's gift of receiving messages from them, he knew that angels were messengers from God, heavenly beings, that also had the assignment of being reapers, collectors of things being sown by man. It has been their assignment to observe mankind. They are recording the words and actions of man to where man will have to give an account one day before God.

In many instances the angels provide unseen aid. They share God's love in many ways by ministering to people in need, by providing necessary provisions or even protections. But they also warn of God's judgment to fall and may be the ones carrying out that judgment. It was also written that they are our escorts to heaven, where we will be in the presence of our Savior.

He discovered that their existence is discussed almost three hundred times in the Bible, and that they had varying ranks, which interested him, it sounded more like military assignments. Which in many cases they are the Host, the Lord's army. There are different job descriptions, messengers to warriors, and those who praise and glorify God. He noted that they remain invisible to most individuals because they are on assignments from God as ambassadors and should not receive praise, our attention should be drawn to the Lord for worship.

It was now pressed on him the importance to know the intent of the angels visiting Emily. It's apparent they were messengers but could they have been there to protect her. Emily had described them as having a dazzling appearance, full of light with beautiful features, they spoke with authority from God. She knew they had great strength and believed them to be powerful, because she had witnessed it at times. She never elaborated on those events. It was something she kept to herself, and he had never pushed for more information. Yet now, he had wished he had spent more time with her, allowing her to talk about her encounters. The angels gave her comfort, knowing they were watching over her, and he was thankful for that. Another gift Emily had was the ability to sense danger, yet she never feared, until now. They had told her that they were there to protect and deliver her from trouble and this she had always trusted in.

The scripture they shared with her was *Psalm 91:11,12 (NASB)*, *"For He will give His angels charge concerning you, To guard you in all your ways. They will bear you up in their hands, That you do not strike your foot against a stone."*

This is exactly what Jim felt had taken place the other night. It was divine surveillance. They were there to deliver a message of warning to him to watch over the girls and to keep them safe, and they knew that Emily could get the message to him. He may have to rely on some of the angels' miraculous deliveries, considering he still doesn't know who to trust.

The scripture that ran through his head was *Matthew 18:10 (NASB)*, *"See that you do not despise one of these little ones, for I say to you that their angels in heaven continually see the face of My Father who is in heaven."*

God had delivered them from the dark events of the past few days. Jim was going to remain calm and rely on God for protection, for he knew that there were many eyes watching over them. He was grateful for the insight that had been given from God to the angel, to his daughter, and now to him to create a plan. He was glad God was speaking.

His wife was pulling the food from the bag that was left at the front door when he had a sudden impulse of fear.

"Don't eat anything that's not prepackaged and sealed tight. We have to be vigilant about everything right now. Until I talk with Allen again, and verify where these men came from, I don't trust anyone or anything."

"Don't worry dear, it's all packaged. We must feed the girls something. But you are right, we do need to be careful, I will be mindful of that."

She went on to prepare the girls a peanut butter sandwich and opened a can of soda for the girls to share. Then turned to him and asked if he wanted anything. He was too focused to be hungry.

It was within an hour that April came down with a fever. She was vomiting and moaning how her tummy hurt. The First Lady was holding her in her lap and rocking her back and forth, trying to comfort her. She looked into her

CHAPTER FOUR

husbands worried eyes and was feeling the guilt, had she accidently poisoned their daughter?

Emily walked over to April and handed her the feather she had found outside. Calmly sharing, "Remember your guardian angel is with you. He will oversee your healing."

"Emily, what are you talking about, dear."

Her mom wasn't understanding the significance of the feather, but it was seemingly bringing April some comfort. She could feel the tension leaving her body as she was holding her.

"It's just something I was told once." She said nonchalantly. "April found the feather outside, and I told her it was from her guardian angel watching over her." She paused and then said, "I think it would be a good time to pray that Jesus will heal April."

She looked at Emily with such warmth. "You are so right, let's lift prayer now, that she will break this fever and whatever has caused it will leave her body, in Jesus' name. For we know that in all things we are victorious through Him who loved us first. Nothing can separate us from the love of God. And in 1 Peter 2:24 we are told that we are healed by the stripes that Jesus bore for us. It is our place now to believe she is healed."

They all shouted, "We do."

"Good, because in Isaiah 41:10 (NCV) it tells us, *'Don't worry, because I am with you. Don't be afraid, because I am your God. I will make you strong and will help you.'"*

Jim knew she was shaping the girls in their faith. It was important to set an example of trusting the Lord and having confidence that what the Word says is true. These patterns of trust will help develop their thoughts and how they handle challenges in their future. Overcoming things together drew them closer as a family. He looked on his wife with such admiration, and thanked God for such a compassionate, loving woman.

Within an hour her fever had broken, she was leaning on her mom sound asleep. The other two girls had gone to bed. Jim scooped April up and took her to bed as well.

"I don't know what happened. Do you think someone tampered with the food? If it was food poisoning, would we not have all been sick?" She was confused and she had rolled those questions around in her head for the past hour. Feeling like she was responsible somehow.

"Stop punishing yourself, you did nothing wrong. You simply fed your children. She will be fine. She is sleeping comfortably now."

He was trying to comfort her, at the same time trying to process the events in his mind as well. If they had tampered with the food, it was likely from inserting something into the top. April must have gotten the bulk of what was injected into the peanut butter. He couldn't remember if she had gotten the first sandwich or not. He went over and pulled the foil lid from the trash.

"What are you doing, digging in the trash?" She was puzzled by his actions.

"If it was tampered with, maybe we need to have it tested. For now, let's stick with things that would be harder to tamper with. Maybe we can find a grocery store somewhere nearby and purchase our own food."

"How long do you think we are going to be here?"

"Maybe shorter than we think. If these men mean harm, then we need to find another way out. They could have simply been handed these things and told to bring them up to us." He was shaking his head. "I just don't know."

"It's been a stressful day and I know you need some rest."

"Yes, I need rest, but I need answers. I'm going to call Allen on that phone they gave us and let him know what took place. It may be nothing or it may lead to something. God only knows the answers to all this. But I know I won't be getting any rest, so you go ahead and get some sleep. You have to find the energy to keep up with the girls."

CHAPTER FOUR

"My body has crashed, but my head is whirling. I doubt there will be sleep."

"I understand. I'll be right in after I make this call." He was encouraging her to go to bed and at least try to sleep.

He dug around for the phone and made the call to Allen. It was later than he had realized. Allen wasn't picking up, so he left a message. That was going to have to be good enough for now. Was he being paranoid? If he got a few hours of rest, maybe he could think more clearly. If these men came out to harm them, wouldn't they have already done so? After all, they are outnumbered. Could April have just been stressed from the events of the day? Maybe she just caught a bug? He reflected on the feather she had found; it might have been nice if we all found feathers on the ground.

He turned the bathroom light on, not wanting to disturb his wife. She had finally given into her exhaustion. As the dim light gently crossed the bed revealing his wife's beauty, he was reminded again how lucky he was to have her. He felt the burden of the events from the previous days and the turmoil that it has caused in their lives. Was being in such a position of power worth all this pain?

Song "Hold On To Me" by Lauren Daigle

Chapter Five

The Warning

It was in the wee hours of the morning, before dawn broke, when Emily felt the presence of something on her shoulder. She woke, first thinking it was June, who was sleeping next to her, who tends to like to snuggle close to her sister April. Because April had not been feeling well, it was thought that she should sleep alone in another room, precautions if it was a bug. Emily reached around to remove June's hand when she realized it wasn't June. It was an angel.

Emily didn't typically carry-on conversations with the angels that appeared to her, she simply listened to the message, but she was curious about the feather, if it had brought healing to April. And she was concerned about the danger they have found themselves in. Circumstances had changed and she was emboldened. She knew to be precise in asking her questions, angels didn't linger. Words delivered from angels were usually Scriptural and would take unraveling to understand, but they were deliberate in their delivery, and they moved on.

"Did you leave the feather for April?" Came rolling off her tongue.

"Yes, it was an assurance that all would be okay." It was felt that Emily would understand that.

"Why not stop her from getting sick?"

"Man is iniquitous."

"What does that mean?"

"Evil."

"So, there was someone evil involved?"

"Yes."

"Can you explain?"

"I have come to deliver a message for your father. Listen carefully and you will find answers. It is true that these are turbulent times, where men have failed to follow their destiny as children of God. The world has allowed totalitarianism to capture humanity without resistance. This breeds poverty, disease, moral decay, and brings about wars. The earth will cry out through earthquakes, eruptions, and unprecedented weather conditions. These things are spoken about in Luke 21. Heed the warnings and focus on the verse in Luke 21:15-19 (NKJV).

'For I will give you a mouth and wisdom which all your adversaries will not be able to contradict or resist. You will be betrayed even by parents and brothers, relatives and friends; and they will put some of you to death. And you will be hated by all for My name's sake. But not a hair of your head shall be lost. By your patience possess your souls.'"

"What about the danger we are in?" She was getting anxious and again felt the insecurity of their safety.

"Tell him that by making the choice to follow Jesus Christ, he has received the protective watch and care of angels. He has been given his appointment; his assignment is to change the events. Thirst for righteousness."

In an instant the angel was gone. She had more questions that didn't get to be asked and she remained confused. Feeling the pressures of her assignment that was not fully understood, she knew that her Dad would want more answers to guide them. This was an urgent message that couldn't wait to be written down. She dashed over to her father's room and tapped on the door. Her parents were sleeping lightly, as if on high alert. She was quickly summoned into the room.

"I have another report." She announced breathlessly. "I haven't written it down yet."

"That's fine, you can tell us about it." They were both anxiously waiting to hear what she had to say.

"You were correct in thinking April was poisoned. I wasn't given any details, just that it was someone evil involved."

Her mother gasped, and her father threw off the covers. He motioned for Emily to come closer. He knew she needed a hug; this was frightening information she was asked to deliver.

He patted the side of the bed and said, "Sit down and tell me more."

She proceeded to recite everything the angel had stated. You could see her squinting, trying to recall every detail through her anxiousness. He nodded trying to take it all in. Wishing he had a Bible close by, to open to the Scripture references, to see if there were any other clues that would help him unravel this message.

"Emily, I know it's early, but I think it would be best if you would find some paper and write everything down while it is still fresh in your mind. I know I am going to need to spend some time thinking about what you delivered to us. Don't disturb your sisters, nor do you need to share any of this with them. It would be upsetting to them. I'm so sorry that this has you in turmoil as well, but you know how helpful this information is to us."

Emily understood what he was saying, and she knew it was best to get everything written down. The message given was not fully understood by Emily, but she was aware of evil being perpetrated on them. She left the room to follow through with his request.

The minute Emily left the room The First Lady burst into tears. "Why are they doing this to us? Who is behind all this, Jim?"

"I'm not sure, but there is a warning in that word, that we can't trust anyone. We may be fighting this battle on our own."

She was shaking uncontrollably. He reached around and held her tight recognizing the stress she was under. Realizing it had been his decision to run for office, feeling responsible for the danger they were in. Although they had agreed on this path, they never thought that they would be putting their lives on the line.

"It's going to be all right. The word said not a hair on our heads will be touched. We have God on our side, honey, there is no one mightier than our God. And it's apparent that He wants us to know what is taking place. After all, our daughter speaks to angels."

As he held his wife close, comforting her, he was also planning their next move.

As his wife showered, trying to wash away the fears that seemed to engulf her, she reflected on the fact that they are being watched over by heavenly beings. She was reminded that her daughter talks with angels. Her husband glorifies God and has a righteous walk among men. Surely, they are blessed and should take comfort in the Lord's protections. After all He is Jehovah Jireh, the Lord our Provider and Jehovah Tsaba, our Warrior, the one fighting our battles, as well as Jehovah Nissi, our Victor. She could take comfort in all that. The tension eased from her body as if it were floating down the drain.

Jim was thinking back on how he got here. Not here, to this house, but how did he arrive at the position he was in. When was it that he decided to run for office of President? This was a position of authority, and with that kind of power there is danger. He had to have known that there would be threats on their lives. Had he brushed that off, because it was a thrill to be seated as the President of a nation, not just a president of a corporation. He was feeling the pressure and responsibility for the dangerous situation he had put his family in. Wondering if he needed to ask forgiveness of some kind of pride in his life that had brought them to this point.

It was Allen who had approached him with the idea to run for office. They had many talks over drinks regarding the condition of the nation and its deterioration. It had been discussed that the nation needed to go back to the days of Benjamin Franklin, when the delegates were challenged to pray before sessions, seeking God's guidance in all things. They had agreed that God is where our help comes from, as it was then, it is today as well. The nation was once grounded, as it was founded in biblical principles and sound judgements. Where had we gone wrong? Why were they living with such confusion? It was time to reestablish "One Nation Under God," lest we be judged from our God above.

They had agreed to fight this battle together. The platform they used was to, "Find common ground," that reflected the interest of the people. Stating that "We need not be so divided that nothing can be decided." They emphasized, when making directives that they should align with Godly principals, so as not to be judged from God. Psalm 50:6 (NKJV) was used in their speeches, *"Let the heavens declare His righteousness, For God Himself is Judge."*

The whole Psalm was used many times in his speeches, he could still almost recite the whole thing, because it came from his heart. *"The Mighty One, God the LORD, Has spoken and called the earth From the rising of the sun to its going down. Out of Zion, the perfection of beauty, God will shine forth. Our God shall come, and shall not keep silent; A fire shall devour before Him, And it shall be very tempestuous all around Him. He shall call to the heavens from above, And to the earth, that He may judge His people: 'Gather My saints together to Me, Those who have made a covenant with Me by sacrifice.' Let the heavens declare His righteousness, For God Himself is Judge. Hear, O My people, and I will speak, O Israel, and I will testify against you; I am God, your God* (Psalm 50:1-7 NKJV)*!"*

He pondered for a moment, reminded that he did make a covenant with God and this country, was he living out his sacrifice?

Pleading with God, "May my sacrifice not involve my family, Lord." And whispering to himself. *"'For the world is Mine, and all its fullness. Offer to God thanksgiving, And pay your vows to the Most High. Call upon Me in the day of trouble; I will deliver you, and you shall glorify Me* (Psalm 50:12,14,15 NKJV).'"

He stopped again and realized that was the word he was needing. Had God led him to that verse for this very moment. He started to glorify God and thank Him for everything that He had blessed Him with: His provision, His guidance, His protections, His blessing, and His deliverance. He had made the decision to run for office and vowed to declare God's righteousness to the people, just like the angel said, man failed his destiny as children of God, and it was his assignment to bring them back around.

This Scripture had been a reminder. He told himself in an audible voice so that the angels could hear him. "Yes, God, I know that you will find a way to deliver us from this trouble."

He then reflected on the Word that he and Allen had covered many times at rallies to try to awaken the public. *"But to the wicked God says: 'What right have you to declare My statutes, Or take My covenant in your mouth, Seeing you hate instruction And cast My words behind you? When you saw a thief, you consented with him, And have been a partaker with adulterers. You give your mouth to evil, And your tongue frames deceit. You sit and speak against your brother; You slander your own mother's son. These things you have done, and I kept silent; You thought that I was altogether like you; But I will rebuke you, And set them in order before your eyes. Now consider this, you who forget God, Lest I tear you in pieces, And there be none to deliver; Whoever offers praise glorifies Me; And to him who orders his conduct aright I will show the salvation of God* (Psalm 50:16-23 NKJV)."

He pondered the Word that he just finished rolling around in his head. There it was again, those words, *"You sit and speak against your brother."* That is somehow tied to the angel's message, *"You will be betrayed even by parents and brothers, relatives and friends."* Who am I being betrayed by? Someone in my cabinet? My counselors? A friend? Or is it just a rouge agent who is supposed to be protecting us? The Word also states that God will reveal this person and deal with them. It is my job to remain faithful. He would need to share these concerns with his wife as soon as she stepped from the shower. It was time to take an offensive measure and be proactive. God was giving him a renewed strength.

The First Lady reentered the bedroom refreshed and glowing. He noticed her beauty, but also her countenance had changed.

"The shower must have agreed with you, my dear." Smiling with a big Cheshire cat smile.

She totally ignored his advancements and simply stated. "It did. It was as if God washed all my anxiety away. I was reminded that we are not alone."

The President proceeded to share with his wife all that had been revealed to him that morning. The verse that came to mind was Isaiah 33:22(NKJV). *"'For the LORD is our Judge, The LORD is our Lawgiver, The LORD is our King; He will save us.'"*

"I understand, 'He will save us,' but why is your focus on the other parts of that verse." She was wanting more explanation.

"We have to recognize Him as King over all things. Including what's happening to us right now. He is revealing things that are hidden from us. Don't lawyers reveal truths through a process? Yes, we are in danger, but there is a root to that danger that we don't know about. It will work its way to the surface, and we will be able to expose who and what it's about and deal with it. But we are also told that, He has the power and authority to judge. God has set up laws for us to follow and He will bring down the gavel on those that have undermined His agenda. God knows our agenda, to bring this country back to His covenant, and He is assisting us in getting it done."

He continued. "In Job 12:22,23(NKJV), *'He uncovers deep things out of darkness, And brings the shadow of death to light. He makes nations great, and destroys them; He enlarges nations, and guides them.'* We used that verse a lot in bringing people around to our thinking. God has the power to birth nations and destroy them. It has been our plan to align ourselves with Him so that He will bless us once again."

"So, you think He is shaking out the snake in the wood pile? And that's why we are finding ourselves on the run?" She questioned.

"Yep, I think that has something to do with it. They could have been trying to perpetrate fear upon us at the house, from the very beginning, with the night of terror. Shake us up, get our minds off our agenda. Pull us away from some important issues being voted on."

"Wait, are you trying to say that all this has been scare tactics? That no one is really trying to kill us? It's just to get us on the run as a distraction, for us and the country?"

"Maybe. I know we were the ones being shot at, but no one was hit. Do you not find that rather odd? These are skilled marksmen."

"But what about Tom, who was killed, and the poison?"

"Could be she just got sick, we haven't had anything analyzed. The girls have been through a lot the past few days. And I haven't forgotten Tom."

"I think you are missing a key factor in all this." She was thinking spiritually now.

"What do you mean?"

"The angels." She stated matter of factually.

"I haven't forgotten, in fact I've been praying all morning. I've been praising God for his protections and provisions, and the angels are a big part of the provision."

CHAPTER FIVE

"Well, they are the ones who have been giving words of warnings. Warnings, dear. And I believe they have been protecting us from harm."

She was getting a little aggravated at her husband. Why was he suddenly wanting to dismiss the supernatural help they had received? What was going on in his head?

She went on to stress, "Crimes are being committed here, and I for one feel that we have been in danger. Remember Emily's warning, that she felt danger lurking."

"I'm not saying we haven't experienced danger and that it may still be out there. I'm just saying that it may all be a distraction for something else going on. Maybe the angels were here to tell us not to feel threatened by all this. I was told to stick with the plan, so to speak."

It was time to be honest with the girls. They sat the girls down to explain what they thought was going on. Whatever the reason for the events that have occurred, they need to remain vigilant and watchful. He assured them that things would be fine.

June was showing some fear mounting in her little body, it began to shake uncontrollably. Jim grabbed her up and asked April to hand him a blanket, he thought she was going into shock. He wrapped her up and held her tight.

"We are all going to be all right, I want you to stay calm. You know that God is with us and has protected us, He is not going to leave us today nor tomorrow."

April asked, "Are we in trouble because you are the President?"

"Could be." He was shaking his head agreeing with his child's conclusion. "Look, people in power have to deal with a lot of different kinds of threats from people who don't agree with them. Difficult decisions are being made every day and they are being pulled in different directions. I like to think that I'm on the side of the Lord, and I'm trying to bring the country back in line with His ways. This may have upset some people."

"Do all Presidents get threats?"

"Most likely, they do. But when they are aligned with God, God protects them. Let me tell you about a President that had supernatural protections from God."

"Kind of like us, huh." Emily stated with a smile.

"Yes, we have experienced some of that ourselves. These protections were demonstrated when God intervened in George Washington's life."

"He was our First President!" shouted April.

Jim smiled, pleased that she remembered that fact. "Yes, and during the French and Indian War, Colonel George Washington was shielded from harm during battle. Although, all the other officers on horseback were shot, and two of his own horses were shot, he was not. It's said that he had four bullet holes in his coat, but nothing struck his body. God had intervened."

Emily stated, "That sounds like what happened to us at the cabin. Gun shots, but nothing penetrated the car."

Jim decided it was best to continue his story versus responding to their event.

"God also intervened in birthing this nation with supernatural weather events."

"What do you mean?" April was surprised to hear that God could control the weather.

"Miracles. During the Revolutionary war, there were British forces outnumbering our troops. They had us surrounded. Our army was waiting for the British to cut off their escape, they knew it was going to take place with all those ships out at sea. The wind died down and the ships were unable to sail. Rain rolled in and George Washington maneuvered his men across the river safely, under the cloak of darkness. Additional cover came when a mysterious fog settled over the army, allowing George and his troops to escape. Now that's what we call the providential hand of God."

CHAPTER FIVE

"Will we see God's providential hand?" April asked wide eyed.

"I think we have been experiencing it already." He winked at Emily. She understood what he meant by that comment.

"Girls, you can see that God will take care of us. I think He is making plans right now how to shield us from harm, just like he shielded George Washington. God shows up at extraordinary times all throughout the Bible. Remember the events your mom shared with you about Joseph, going from the pit to the top position, running Egypt. How about the fiery furnace, Jesus showed up there and the guys came out smelling like a rose."

The girls giggled, "They did not."

"Well, they didn't smell like smoke. And what about the big event at the Red Sea."

"Yeah, God parted the water, and they walked across on dry land." The girls shouted all together with big smiles. Their mother had been doing a fine job teaching the girls the events in the Bible.

"See, you do know where God has been, and He is still working today. He hasn't changed. Psalm 102:27,28 (NKJV) tells us, *'But You are the same, And Your years will have no end. The children of Your servants will continue, And their descendants will be established before You.'* So, we shouldn't fear anything."

The girls gathered around him and gave him a big hug. His wife looked on in admiration, thinking, I'll follow that man anywhere he goes.

Song "Yes He Can" by CAIN

Chapter Six

Getting Close

The man that had been in the trunk of the car ended up using the presidential vehicle to drive further than he expected, before ditching it for another vehicle. He had trouble finding a vacated car to apprehend on his path towards Washington. It had surprised him that there had been no attempt to locate the vehicle. Anticipating a deluge of cops at any point and time, he was prepared to talk his way out of trouble. Now that the pressure was off after disposing of the presidential ride, his focus was to find the Vice President, Allen Crandall, and get the information that he needed to find the family.

He knew it wasn't going to be an easy task to get close to the Vice President under any conditions, but considering the events that had been going on, it would be nearly impossible. He had disguised himself as one of the janitors, to move about the offices freely in hopes of uncovering information as to the family's location.

The Vice President was acting suspiciously around some of his aids. It was as if he was trying to keep things from prying eyes. With all the excitement at hand, it was assumed no one should be brought into the inner circle, which made it more concerning that a janitor was able to move through the building with ease. Guess no one likes to take out the trash, were his thoughts, as he dug through the cans, looking for anything that might have a clue as to where the stash house was located, assuming they had been put up somewhere out of sight.

Another trip up the back steps, he hit paydirt. Vice President Crandall was attempting to whisper to someone above him in the stairwell.

He was emphatic with his words, "No mistakes this time."

Apparently, something had gone wrong. Heads were going to roll if anything caused the family to bolt again. "You have to get up there and take care of it."

This was perfect, he thought, I'll follow this fellow right to the family. He left the cans in the stairwell and quietly exited, keeping watch on who came out behind him.

As he followed the agent, he said to himself, "This is like taking candy from a baby."

The President had to devise another plan. He was focusing on the messaging from the Scriptures that the angels had shared. He was to "gain understanding", he was sure that was from the Word. There was something about the use of discretion. Was that not already in his plans on how to move forward? Wasn't he contemplating every move they were making? Noting that they had already experienced the terror of the past few days and realized it's from someone's wicked agenda. The Lord protected them from those events. It was even supernatural how they were able to escape and how April overcame her illness so quickly.

He was recognizing that they definitely had the favor of the Lord on them. Remembering that God says that He blesses the just.

CHAPTER SIX

Contemplating the matter over in his head, "Surely the Lord knows that I am trying to fulfill a promise to Him and to this country, that we will remain 'One Nation Under God.'"

Now reflecting on the report again, it was apparent that he needed to get that other report from Emily. He knew there was more to each of those Words given. His eyes needed to be on each one, to figure out what other warning was left that might protect them from further harm.

The First Lady was trying to keep the girls busy to keep their minds off all the drama that was whirling around them. She was doing a good job entertaining them, while Emily was working diligently on the report.

The President pulled out the first report and was pouring over it again. Was there anything he missed?

"Okay Lord, my eyes are on the message that was given to me. Now, can I hear from you? Clarify anything that I am missing."

He continued to mumble to himself, but he knew he was talking to the Lord.

"There is something, or someone that is a stumbling block. I'm sure that is tied to the betrayal. But who? And is it connected to the oppressor that I am not to envy? Why would I envy anyone? Apparently, that person is ungodly, scornful, and a fool. Well, that's some kind of description. Got any weight, height, ethnic characteristics to share? How about a name?"

He was getting a little punchy and needed to look inward, before offending the Lord. God is a big God and can handle our disagreeable attitudes but it's always best to remember that He is Elohim the Creator, and one should always demonstrate respect for the Most High God.

"I recognize those words Lord, that you provide grace, I might need some of that right now, because I am interested in inheriting some of that glory that is mentioned, as well."

About that time, Emily walked up to hand him the second report. "What is glory?"

"Glory can be a lot of things, baby girl, but mostly it's God's presence. And a lot of good comes from His presence, like peace, understanding, and even healing."

"Are you sick?" She looked puzzled.

"No, but it's funny that the first report mentions keeping Gods words in my heart, that the words are, *'life to those who find them and health to all their flesh* (Proverbs 4:22 NKJV).' Then there were the ones that said, *'diligently keep your heart, for out of it spring the issues of life* (Proverbs 4:23 NKJV).'"

"What does it mean?"

"That's what I'm contemplating on, at least how it applies to our situation right now. I believe it meant that we are to memorize and hold close, God's Word, so that we can live by and use the guidance that He supplied for us in our day-to-day life. If we follow His ways and His advice, we will remain healthy and flourish. Then there is the part, *'out of it spring the issues of life,'* that could mean what's important to us. Still working on it. I know there is a hidden message in there somewhere that's meant for us today."

She handed him the report. "It's finished."

This kind of talk was starting to go way over her head. She was able to deliver messages as the angels told her, but it didn't mean that she understood all that the message was conveying. Key phrases maybe, but not the full impact of what she was relaying to them.

"Thank you, honey."

She was about to walk away, and he asked, "Hey, you think it's possible that I might have a visitation from an angel? The message before mentioned, *'When I lie down, I won't be afraid* (Proverbs 3:24 NKJV),' just wondered if that meant I'm going to be visited."

CHAPTER SIX

"I don't know, Dad. But if you believe, it's possible. Talk to Jesus. Who knows?" She shrugged her shoulders. Wanting to finish up, so that she could play with her sisters.

"Thanks, sweetie, I'll go over this right now." Holding up the second report.

He was back to thinking out loud and talking to the Lord, hoping He would pop in any time, to help solve the issues they were confronted with.

"Issues of the day, that's it, it's my agenda, my platform for the country. My issues revolve around righteousness, justice, and morality for the country. Someone opposed to my agenda is behind all these events. Now, who can I narrow that down to?"

Now that was a rhetorical question that he laughed at, knowing that he had lots of opposition.

He opened Emily's report and the first thing that jumped out at him was the angel's first remark. "Listen carefully and you will find answers!" Pondering, waiting for anything to jump out at him. "Well, I'm listening, but I think what I'm needing is more research."

At that moment, as if perfect timing, his wife walked in holding a Bible. "Look what I found. I was searching the drawers for markers or crayons for the girls, and found this Bible. Would it help in your research?"

"Why yes, it would. In fact, it's just what I needed. If I can't have Jesus face-to-face, I can have His Word." He took the book and opened it directly to Luke 21 and started reading.

He noted verse four where the widow gave all that she had; it reads *"all the livelihood that she had* (Luke 21:4 NKJV)." It occurred to him, that he has given all that he has, to take on this position. He gave up his freedom and liberty to move about on his own, without security following him around, and constantly being watched. He gave up his privacy, everything is published for the public's eye. He left behind his wealth from running a prosperous corporation.

And apparently, he gave up not only his, but his family's security and safety. He has sacrificed to be in this position. He still felt he was doing the will of God, trying to bring the country back around in alignment with God.

When the Pilgrims came to America to advance their Christian faith, they persevered much and left a mark for all to see by planting a cross at Cape Henry. Jim and his wife had stated that they wanted to plant a cross in the heart of every home across the nation to advance God's agenda, to preserve what was once started. He was reminded that there is a cost to partner with Christ, but it's worth the price. He reflected on what was said by Jesus himself, in Matthew 16:24-27 (NKJV), *"If anyone desires to come after Me, let him deny himself, and take up his cross, and follow Me. For whoever desires to save his life will lose it, but whoever loses his life for My sake will find it. For what profit is it to a man if he gains the whole world, and loses his own soul? Or what will a man give in exchange for his soul? For the Son of Man will come in the glory of His Father with His angels, and then He will reward each according to his works."*

As he contemplated on what he had sacrificed, he realized he wouldn't change a thing. He then read over verses five and six and tried to apply them to circumstance of the day. The temple in Jerusalem was adorned and visited by many, yet its fate was destruction. Our country was once adorned with beauty. People from around the world desired what this land stood for and what was founded here. The sacrifices of men and women to make this country great, the freedoms that they established with their bloodshed are treasured. The courage and boldness that was beautifully demonstrated draws others to our land.

But the day had come that evil systems tore down what was once built up to be a beacon to others, just as the Romans had destroyed the temple. When he and The First Lady arrived in Washington, their attention was drawn to the amount of corruption taking place in the nation's capital under the noses of constituents as well as partisans. Money laundering schemes were exposed, where many of the politicians were the ones conducting racketeering, and the use of shell companies was a blatant practice. Meaningless charges had been brought up against those caught, but the workings were too deep in the judicial departments to have resolved things at the root of the problem. Cleaning up their nation from corruption and wicked practices was why he ran for office, a desire to restore the nation to its beauty and honor, to shine and be a beacon of hope again. It was supposed to be the demonstration of the land of the free, the redeemed human race, not a pit of corruption and enslavement. They just needed more time.

As he read further into the verses, there seemed to be more clarity. He was getting the warning to not be deceived. Furthermore, he understood it to mean that many may come saying that they are with him and may even quote Scripture, placating to him that they are Believers. Yet, they only intend to deceive, they are working towards his demise and persecution. He was being told not to fear the rumors and commotions of the day yet expect that there will be lots of division in the nation. All of which may bring about shakings and hardships. Look to heaven for signs to guide him.

Grabbing his head in frustration "Which I have been doing Lord, I'm seeking your Word, I'm getting reports from angels, and I'm trying to apply the wisdom from Scripture."

He read on and focused on the Scripture the angel pointed out, verse fifteen. "*For I will give you a mouth and wisdom which all your adversaries will not be able to contradict or resist.* (Luke 21:15 NKJV)."

"Well, you must be talking about truth, the truth sets us free. The truth can't be denied, it always breaks through and casts light on darkness, causing it to flee. I know your truth Lord, but I'm also seeking specific truths about what's going on here." He hadn't given up talking to the Lord directly.

His wife came in to check on him. "It's getting kind of rowdy in here; you need some company?"

"Well, you did say, you're filled with wisdom, please come in and have a seat. Two heads are better than one. And I've had no visitation."

"Visitation?" She looked puzzled by that comment.

"Yeah, I got the notion that I might be getting a visitation from an angel. And if I sat here long enough pouring over the Word maybe I could make it happen."

"Might want to leave that one alone for a while." She smiled with a little hesitation.

"I've been trying to apply the verses to our situation, as if it's like a code to be revealed. Honestly honey, it's difficult."

He was getting a little more frustrated stating it out loud to her. He'd wrap his head around one point and then get bogged down by another. He was glad that his wife decided to help, a new perspective on things could shed some light in the right direction.

"Hope you aren't distorting the Word, dear."

"I'm not meaning to; I just feel there is a message to be decoded in all this." He proceeded to cover some of what he had so far.

Adding some key elements. "I believe our safety is in being patient. The angel said they're watching. Look here, where it states that I was given this appointment, President, I assume, and I have an assignment to change events. Isn't that what I am trying to do?"

"Don't leave out the part about thirst for righteousness. Thirst would be defined as a strong desire for something, as if you can't quench the desire. Righteousness is moral correctness, upright and justifiable." She was reading over his shoulder and adding what came to mind.

"Yeah, we always considered it God's path, laid out for us to walk with Him. Okay, that's the platform we are following, we are trying to move the country back to God's desired ways."

"Maybe we are to get the country to desire it. They need to thirst for it."

"Okay, how else are we to proceed?"

"Honey, that's for you and Allen to work on together. What did the other verses say that you were reading outside the report?"

"Oh, 'surrounded by armies, desolation is near.'"

Her eyes got big, and she cocked her head to the side. "Is that meant for us?"

"I don't know. I don't know what's happening in DC either. We have been cut off from the world being out here."

"That may have been by design. What else is in there?" Trying to take a fresh look at it.

"Something about fleeing to the mountains, which apparently, we have done. It goes on to say, 'Woe to the pregnant and those nursing' because of the great distress in the land. Talks about being captive, which feels like our predicament." He looked in her direction and asked the question. "You aren't pregnant, are you?"

"Of course not." She smiled, realizing that would have to be an immaculate conception, because they had tried for years and had not been blessed with a pregnancy. She was considered barren, which is why they adopted three beautiful girls.

"Well, apparently, we are looking at some very stressful times."

She was feeling the stress, and she knew she wasn't alone. It was written all over her husband's face. She watched him light up when he thought he discovered something in the Word and then fall back down from the weight of all the unknown.

"Yes, it mentions something about times being fulfilled."

"I think it's time for us to create our own plans for escaping this. I don't know who to trust. But I go back to what I've said before, we have to trust someone."

"Maybe trust but verify." She said realizing that it was key to verify before sharing information to anyone.

"You are a wise woman."

Chapter Seven

Converging Events

Jim, President Patterson, figured he needed to focus on the message from the angel. There were words warning of danger, warnings of betrayals, encouragement to stick with the assignment he was given, to avoid impending stressful times for the nation. What concerned him was the danger the girls might be in. Someone had tried to get in their room the night before the party. Then Tom was shot the next day, that was a different threat. Or was it? Did they discover our trip plans and were wanting to hijack the car with the girls in it? Or did Tom see another threat, something going down, and tried to stop it, which led to his death? Were these converging events or all connected? Time to call Allen, to see what he had been able to find out about the threats.

"Allen, you have been a difficult man to get a hold of." Jim stated, a little aggravated considering the danger that his family was in.

"It's been crazy around here, Jim. No one knows how the media got hold of the threats. So, DC is buzzing, and the country is concerned, of course. Don't worry, I have a handle on it."

"Gee, it was our hope that people thought we were just on vacation. Which was the original plan. Surely you can trace the leak?"

"I'm on it." Allen stated with confidence.

"Look, we are needing information regarding these threats. Who is behind them? What are they asking for? Has anyone come forward demanding anything?"

"No, no one."

"How well did you vet these men up here?"

"Why, has something else happened?"

"I left you a message. Did you not get it?"

"No. What happened?" Realizing he should have been on top of this.

"We believe my daughter was poisoned."

"What? Why on earth would you think that?"

"She was very sick last night, after eating some of the food sent up here."

"That might just be a coincidence, Jim. Children get sick. Maybe the stress."

"I don't know. Answer the question about the men, Allen. Are we safe?" Jim was letting his temper get out of hand.

"Yes, they are all good men. I personally vetted them. You are safe." There was a pause. "I'm sure you are fine. The stress is getting to all of you."

"Oh, I'm not stressed, I'm determined. Determined to get to the bottom of all this."

"We both are. Now let me handle my end. You stay with your family. I'll send more food, tamper resistant food your way. If that makes you feel better." Thinking that's the way it was handled before.

"Watch your step Allen, that sounds a bit condescending."

"Never. You know I am just trying to take care of you. We go way back, Jim. You can trust me."

Jim paused trying to calm himself. There was that word, trust. "I do. Thanks. I know you are having a tough time as well. Sorry about that, I guess I am a little stressed." His voice began to accelerate, "You know my family's lives are in danger. Now, I want reports on the threats ASAP! You got that?"

Allen was a little flustered by Jim's remarks, but he took it in stride and promised to report back soon.

The man from the trunk followed the agent up the mountain to where the family was taking refuge. The agent had stopped to unhook the chain across the dirt road when a car came up from behind and hit him. The man got out quickly and moved the lifeless agent to the ditch, first taking his phone, badge, and keys. He parked his vehicle a little further down the road and came back to the agent's car, assuming the other surveillance at the house would recognize this type of vehicle, and possibly wouldn't cause a stir. What he realized was that he would likely be stopped at some point. The thought ran through his head that he would just mow the other agents down as well, then run the car into the front of the house.

When he noticed the bag of groceries and thought he had been given another gift. His way to the front door. They would be expecting a delivery. Not being sure how the other agents covering the house would react, or if there would be some kind of roadblock before the final destination. He drove cautiously up the hill. It was best to take it easy. To his satisfaction and surprise, he drove right up to the front of the house, got out slowly, tipped his hat like he was expected, grabbed the bag, and walked up the steps. Thinking to himself, this is too easy.

His heart was beating fast, he was so close now. He knocked and the President was the one who came to the door.

"Who sent you?" Came from the authoritative voice.

"Allen."

"Just drop the bag and back away."

"Sir, I can bring things in for you and set them up. I'm here to help. Is there anything else you need?" His roadblock had begun, and he needed to push through.

"No, thank you. Now, step away." The President was empathic.

This guy was being too chatty, unlike the other agent. Red flags were going off in Jim's head. He motioned for his wife to open the door and grab the bag, while he had the gun pointed at the guy's head.

Out of desperation, this man was going through with his plans. He was going to have to move quick, or he was either going to get a bullet in his back from agents or from the front, facing the President. He held a gun behind the bag. As the door opened, he pushed his way in and grabbed the First Lady, brandishing his weapon.

"Now, put that pea shooter down, nobody needs to get hurt." He felt in charge now.

This took them all off guard. Jim hadn't actually thought that the agent would attack, not after the remarks from Allen. The girls squealed, then got quiet very fast, when the intruder looked in their direction. Where are the other agents? Was flashing through Jim's mind. To the intruder's surprise there was no other agent inside with the family.

The First Lady was shouting in her head, "shoot him, shoot him Jim", you could see it in her eyes. Her only concern was the girls. Jim was a good shot and she felt he could handle him. If he gave up his weapon, she knew they would have lost any hope of advantage.

"You know, you are outmanned. I fire off a shot, and all the agents will come running in." Jim spoke up boldly hoping to rattle him a little.

"Yes, but who exactly is running in to aid you? Can you trust them? How do you know that it's not what they have been waiting for? An opportunity to kill the whole family." The intruder snapped back, rattling them more than he was moved by the comments.

"What are you talking about? You are the one holding the gun on my family."

"But I'm not here to kill anyone."

"You're holding a gun to my ribs." The First Lady stated sarcastically.

"Well, let me clarify for you, I don't want to kill anyone."

"I believe we have a standoff here; I'm not putting my gun down." The President was firm about his response as he slowly moved towards the girls wanting to shield them.

"Okay, look, I have some information for you, and I am wanting some information from you."

This just confused the President more. While holding my wife hostage, he states that he is not the danger, that it may be the men outside. And that he is after information from us. This was definitely out of the ordinary.

"What kind of information do you have that would interest us?"

"Now, we're getting somewhere. Let's have a seat and get our cards on the table before those goons get suspicious."

"Goons?" The First Lady huffed. "Those men are protecting us."

"Not doing a very good job, are they?" He snipped back at her. "And I did say goons, they are hired help. The kind of help you don't want around." He stated bluntly.

The President broke in. "What are you trying to say?"

"I'm saying I believe they are hired to kill you. Didn't I make myself clear before."

She was shaking her head, "I don't understand."

"That's not my problem lady, I'm not here to make sense of anything, I'm here for information."

"What kind of information are you looking for?" The President shot back in anger.

"I want to know which one of those kids is mine?" He bobbed his head toward the girls.

"What?" Was the surprise response from all of them.

The First Lady shouted with a protective voice. "They are our girls."

"Nope, one of them is mine. And I'd like to know which one, right now."

It was obvious he didn't have a clue as to which girl was his. He must have never laid eyes on her. And it was clear to the President and his wife that it wasn't the twins because he would have known that much. What on earth was he up to? They were having to deduce things quickly before giving anything away.

"Why don't you explain what's going on." The President asked.

"It's a life and death situation I got going on. And I rightly don't care who I take down with me." He threatened.

"All right, we just want to know, what it is you think you need with one of our children?"

Jim was trying to get to the bottom of this man's needs and why he was demanding his child. He was not about to hand over any of his children. He would die protecting them.

"How do you even know if one of our girls is yours?" The First Lady was getting feisty.

"I've done my homework. I know one of them is mine. And I am needing help."

"What kind of help? And stop dragging this out. We need to get to the bottom of this. You said yourself we might be in some other kind of danger."

He paused a minute, rubbed his chin, and said, "You're right, you are in danger. And I need to get what is mine before something else happens."

"What? What else is to happen?" More concern surfaced.

"I know the stuff that went down that night, and the next day."

CHAPTER SEVEN

There was a pause, he realized the cat was out of the bag, he was admitting to trying to break in and almost entering their home. But at this point, what did it matter, he was holding them at gun point. He tickled himself. He chuckled and went on to lay his cards on the table.

"I tried to get into the girl's room, I was going to take DNA samples, you know, some hair, or something like a toothbrush to determine which girl was mine. I know about stuff like that, I'm no dummy. I've heard lots of stories in the pen."

"You're a convict?" The First Lady was flustered but realized how silly a comment that was when he was obviously a criminal.

"Look, I've done time. That's why I've been away. I didn't know I had a child. I would have done right by her. My wife is the one that gave her up. Now she has passed. But it was the family that told me about the baby girl. When I got out, I was going to try to find her, but she was lost in the system, until some clerk finally came around with the truth and told me where she was. I think she thought I was going to pay her, or something. But she knew some rich folks got hold of my girl."

"That doesn't prove a thing." The First Lady spouted back at him.

The girls were wide eyed and taking it all in. They had no idea if they were staring at their biological father, or not, but they knew they didn't want any part of his life. They were a family, and they didn't want to be torn apart.

"I'm looking for the proof, that's why I'm here."

"What kind of information or proof did this woman give you?" Questions were being directed back at him.

"She provided me with the signature of my wife, the date she gave her up. The name of the baby girl." He hesitated and they were all holding their breath. "Emily. Emily is her precious name." He looked over at the girls and asked, "Which one of you is Emily?"

Jim and his wife were holding their breath hoping that Emily wouldn't step forward. Keep this man questioning. The First Lady was desperately trying to make eye contact with Emily, her eyes screaming "no, don't respond!"

Emily stepped forward; she wasn't showing any fear. She knew everything was going to be all right. What no one else knew was that she had her eyes on her angel. The angel was nodding, as if all was going to be fine.

"No." The First Lady said breathlessly shaking her head gently.

"It's okay, mom. Everything will be okay." Out of the mouth of babes. She was trying to comfort her mother.

"I knew it." The intruder was expressing some relief. "I thought you looked like your mother."

"What do you want with me?" Emily asked sympathetically. "I have a family, and I am happy. Why would you want to destroy that?"

"I don't. I don't want to destroy anything. I just want a chance at life." You could see the sadness and desperation in his face. It almost brought tears to the girls.

"A life with me?" Emily asked.

"If that's a possibility, then yes. But I am not here to take you from your family. I have a rare disease and I am looking for a donor to give me life. Much of my life has been spent behind bars and I am finally free now. I just want to live." He sounded desperate.

"What would you need from Emily?" Came from the worried mother.

"Blood, possibly a kidney." Stated as if those things are just easily bartered.

"That would have to be her decision." Jim said emphatically.

"True, I'd never force her to do anything. I just wanted to find her and ask her, if she would be willing to help her father live."

"Don't tests have to be run to determine matches?"

"Yes, they do. Can you see the pickle I'm in? I had to find my daughter, I needed to see if she was willing to help me. And to my surprise, she is tied

CHAPTER SEVEN

to the most prominent family in the nation. I didn't think I could just waltz into the White House and declare my needs. I'm kind of used to finding other avenues to get the job done, if you know what I mean."

All eyes were on Emily. It was a monumental burden to ask, what this man was asking of a child. What a horrible time for this to be dumped on them. The family was facing so many obstacles and dangers. Silence had fallen in the room. You could hear a pin drop.

Jim finally asked the question, that hadn't been answered. "You seemed to know of the danger that we are all in, can you explain what it is, and how you know it?"

"Oh yes, I hid from the agents watching the big house. By the way you need better agents. The next day, I saw the driver taken out, shot right in the head."

There were gasps from the girls. They had not been told about Tom's death. The First Lady looked disgusted at his revealing this information to the girls. She was unable to comfort her girls at this moment which was crushing her spirit.

"My bad, I didn't know that they were unaware. But it's time to face reality here. You have a hit on you."

There it was, the plain truth of the matter, spilled out from a man with a gun on them. Now they needed to process what he had just dumped on them. It was their new reality that they needed to face, promptly.

"What?" Asked the President. "I know we have been shot at, we thought maybe it was just a scare tactic. We assumed they were trying to kidnap the girls for ransom of some sort."

"Well, you thought wrong." He stated flatly. "I know a hit attempt when I see one. And you have a target on your back, sir. Maybe I was trying to save my girl from the circle you find yourself in. Because it's a real circle of trouble."

By this time, the guns had been dropped, the girls were huddled together, and the adults in the room were trying to put their heads together, to come up with a scenario of what was happening.

He was saying the obvious out loud. "At least we have two guns to fight them off, now."

"So, you are saying, you were there the night the girls were screaming, when the big commotion started? And you were present when Tom was killed?"

"I was present, but I didn't witness it."

"You just said you saw it happen."

"Not exactly. I said, I saw that he was taken out. May have come out wrong. By the time I came on the scene he was dead. I just took my place in the trunk of the car to follow the family. I think there was a convergence of activity going on at your house that day. I didn't mean any harm, but someone was meaning to get a shot off at you. I think the driver saw something and was taken out. It probably led to a delay in the plans they had for you."

"What about the shots fired at the cabin?" He was trying to unravel the events.

"That wasn't me. They weren't even shooting at me; I was in the trunk. Trust me I was surprised they couldn't bring the car down somehow with all those shots. I was fearing they'd hit the gas tank or something."

Jim was thinking the same thing his wife was thinking. They were protected by the angels watching over them.

"So, you think they were purposefully trying to kill us then?"

"Dang straight. They'd been able to cover it up too. Trust me, them guys know how to cover their tracks."

"Why do you think these agents out here are connected with those guys?"

"It's a brood of snakes for sure." He was shaking his head like it all made sense.

CHAPTER SEVEN

Jim was not sure about trusting this fellow, but he was connecting some dots. He wanted an opportunity to talk to his wife alone, but he didn't see that as an option right now. He was going to have to think quick, their lives depended on it. When it occurred to him that he had not asked all the questions that he needed to ask.

"How did you find us up here?" Jim continued his questioning.

"I heard you talking about the Vice President, so when you ditched the car, I went straight to him."

"He told you where we were?" Jim was a bit shocked.

"Not exactly. I overheard him talking with the agent that I followed up here."

"Where is that agent?"

"In a ditch."

"You killed him?"

"No, I ain't going back to jail for that. I just ran him over. He should be okay." He stated nonchalantly, not really sure one way or the other.

Jim threw his head back and moaned "Who am I dealing with here? Does he not realize all the crimes he has already admitted to?" It was almost laughable, but it's not.

"I imagine we are running out of time then. Someone is going to spot the body, or he is going to wake up and look for assistance."

"Sure, that's probably what's going to happen. So how are we going to handle this? I still need some answers from my girl over there." He looked in Emily's direction.

"If we can get to a lab, I'll have some tests run. We can see if it's true, that she is your daughter. Then we can discuss with her what she wants to do. No need to put that pressure on her right now. The pressure is for us all to survive whatever attack is coming our way."

"I can get on board with that." He humbly said, "Thank you for even listening to me."

"We may be the ones thanking you if what you say is right. You want to share a name?"

"George. That's all you need to know for now."

"Okay, George it is."

Jim started looking out the windows, trying to spot one of the agents. Are they really watching the house? Where are they? Were they not suspicious of this man coming inside? Maybe they are expecting him to attack us, and they are the clean-up crew.

George spoke up. "Wondering where they are, aren't you? I questioned that myself after the first few minutes I arrived. They may have fallen for me coming in and putting things away, maybe. But this length of time? They should know that something is up, they should have showed their hand by now." He paused, shook his head, and followed with, "Can't trust hired help."

"Apparently, I can't trust anyone." Jim was furious.

"I thought it was kind of fishy, how that Allen guy was talking with that agent in the stairwell."

"What was said?" Jim's curiosity was piqued.

"He was pretty aggravated. It was something like, No mistakes this time. Take care of it."

Jim didn't know how to respond to that. It could mean something about the food, something about the men he hired. He just didn't know for sure. It could go either way.

"You got a beef with your VP there, big guy?"

"No, we are old friends. I don't know what he meant by that. He is on my side. He is the one that got me into the Presidency."

"Oh, I see."

"What do you mean by that?"

"He couldn't get there on his own, so he is riding your coattails." He seemed to have it all figured out.

Jim was shaking his head, what was he getting at.

"It happens to the best of us, you ride along with someone else until it's your turn to lead." It made perfect sense to George.

"Are you suggesting that my old friend coerced me into running for office, because he needed to ride my coattails into the spotlight? And now he is trying to bump me off, so that he can take the lead."

"You said that perfectly." George was smiling and pleased with himself that he figured out what the President had been unable to see.

"But we are friends, like brothers." He exclaimed in shock, then it hit him.

"Power does weird things to friendships. Take it from me, I know."

Now the Scripture came flooding back. The warning of betrayal from a brother. This was a crushing blow. He looked into his wife's eyes and saw that she was teared up over the pain he was feeling. He was in shock, and she wanted to comfort him, but was afraid to make any sudden moves. Strange things were occurring, they were going to have to trust a man that had them at gun point. But he was making some sense out of the turn of events.

Jim knew that they were needing help, apparently it wasn't coming from friends. It was time to rely totally on God. The Scripture that came to mind was not one he would have thought of on his own, it must have been laid on his heart.

Job 12:4-6 (AMP), *"I am become one who is a laughingstock to his friend; I, one whom God answered when he called upon Him—a just, upright (blameless) man—laughed to scorn! In the thought of him who is at ease there is contempt for misfortune—but it is ready for those whose feet slip. The dwellings of robbers prosper; those who provoke God are [apparently] secure; God supplies them abundantly [who have no god but their own hands and power]."*

Job 12:9-12(AMP), *"Who [is so blind as] not to recognize in all these [that good and evil are promiscuously scattered throughout nature and human life] that it is God's hand which does it [and God's way]? In His hand is the life of every living thing and the breath of all mankind. Is it not the task of the ear to discriminate between [wise and unwise] words, just as the mouth distinguishes [between desirable and undesirable] food? With the ages [you say] is wisdom, and with length of days comes understanding. But [only] with [God] are [perfect] wisdom and might; He [alone] has [true] counsel and understanding."*

Jim was shouting in his head, "Why God? Why has this happened to me? Why such a betrayal? I trusted in the wrong people, I thought he was my friend, and he has made a mockery of me. I should have recognized the signs. You warned me to be wise and I fell short. I trusted my own instincts when I should have sought You out and waited on You. Help us Lord, give us counsel on how to move forward. How do I protect my family?"

George spoke up, breaking Jim's concentration. "I know you got a lot on your mind over there, but we need to have an exit plan. I'm afraid the only one we got is to dash out the door like you did at the cabin. These are different guys; they won't know how it went down. But I can bet they are getting antsy. We got two guns on them now, that's to our advantage."

"The difference is we didn't know for sure if anyone would shoot at us, and it's a given here. And we aren't in a protective vehicle." There was some hesitancy in this decision.

"Yeah, well just consider yourselves experienced." George spoke as if patting them on the back for a job well done.

Jim looked out the window again to see if he spotted anyone moving in their direction. He gathered the girls and his wife close. The plan was to shield them the best he could as they made their way to the car. George was to run

CHAPTER SEVEN

around to the driver's side, leaving him a little more exposed, but he could move swiftly without having to protect anyone but himself.

"It's time to move quickly."

Chapter Eight

The Wrong Target

George couldn't help himself. He pulled out a blade and slashed the other car's tires.

"That will slow them down a bit." He chuckled to himself.

"You're slowing us down. Get in, let's go." Jim shouted.

The agents were running toward the car, pulling their weapons. George spun off and was down the dirt road before they could get a shot off. You could hear them starting their car, but they were going nowhere fast. He drove right through the chains that had been blocking the entrance. Once they hit the main road, George pulled off next to the vehicle he had left earlier.

"Get out, we are switching modes of transportation."

"That's going to be a tight fit, George."

"Naw, it's fine. We can swap down the road a bit. I'd rather not be spotted in this thing. They know the make and model." He was insisting that they move fast.

They all piled out of the agent's car and crawled into the smaller car that he had driven up the mountain. No need for seatbelts, they were packed in there like sardines.

The First Lady had been so proud of the girls. They had not complained once. They remained silent and calm. She was a little concerned about how quiet Emily had been over the whole shock of this man claiming to be her father, along with the threat they were all under.

She reached around and hugged Emily and started patting her hair. Emily was comforted by her mother's gentle touch and knew she was worried about her.

"Mom, I'm okay. We are all okay." She was trying to encourage her mom.

"Yes, we are, honey. We are all okay."

She turned to look straight at her mother and whispered, "My angel is here."

"Right now?" She was looking around. "How?"

"He's on the hood." She smiled.

"Well, that's good, because I don't think there's room for even a feather in here."

They giggled. The others turned to see what was so funny.

"It's an inside joke." For some reason that got them all tickled, and the car was filled with laughter.

After about thirty minutes of driving, they spotted another car that would be more accommodating. It was a quick stop, hotwire, and off they went.

"You got some skill there, George." Jim was congratulating him on the speed of his work.

"Yeah, it would be part of the reason I was in the slammer."

"Well, I'll make sure you don't end up in there again. Where are we headed?"

"I'm headed to the lab, you promised me. I need to know those results."

"Actually, that's a good idea. I have something of my own I want tested."

The First Lady knew what he was talking about, she simply asked, "You got it?"

"Yep. And I will need it as proof." It was clear that he was building a case.

The sun was setting, and George knew they wouldn't reach the lab tonight. Before he left DC, he had scoped out all the labs within a hundred miles. Once he had the DNA needed, he was heading to one of those labs. For now, he would look for a place to stay that wouldn't draw attention.

June's tummy rumbled so loud it set off a series of tummies growling. It was time to feed these children. There had been very little to eat in the past two days. An apple had been all they could find to eat this morning. Being on high alert with all the activity that had occurred takes away one's appetite. But now that things were calmer and they were getting some answers to their many questions and on a secure path, it left room for one's mind to go to other considerations, like hunger.

George said, "I got this. I'm sure we all need some food, not just the little one back there."

He pulled into the drive-through at the first fast-food establishment he came to. Rolling up to the kiosk he was about to place an order for the occupants of the car.

Noticing Jim pulling out his wallet to cover the dinner, George was gracious and piped in, "I got this, don't worry, I'm sure you aren't used to carrying around cash. You know you can't use credit cards?"

"Thanks George. I had used just about all my cash the other day. And yes, I knew not to use the credit cards. Have you got enough to put us up for the night. We can all stay in one room. I will reimburse you for all the expenses."

"Yeah, I got it covered. Don't be expecting any first-class hotel."

He rolled down the window at the mic and ordered off the dollar menu. "I'll take a dozen of those small cheeseburgers, five small fries, five cups of water and a chocolate milk." He paused then added with a smile, "I'm feeling generous tonight, throw in six of those apple pies."

Jim was smiling at his generosity, not making a sound over his dinner choices. George turned to Jim as he was pulling forward to the window to pay, giving him instructions.

"Now, you look out the window that way, and ma'am you keep your head down. These folks probably have no idea who you are, but I don't want to take any chances."

As George pulled up to the window, he started chatting up the girl to take her mind off who she might see in the car. He was a talker and had sufficiently captured her attention.

"Hey honey, this is highway robbery with these here prices. When did things get so expensive? Or is it just that way up here in the north?"

It worked, the girl was flustered and just starting giggling. After all, it was less than thirty dollars for a bag full of food. George grabbed the bag, took the milk out and handed the rest to Jim to dispense.

"Don't you want a burger, George."

"Heck no, I don't eat that trash." He paused, then said, "But I'll take one of those pies."

Jim was starting to like this fellow. It occurred to him that he was living in a Stockholm syndrome scenario. Although he wasn't sure who had whom for hostage. He had not come after them with the intent to harm. He was the one needing something from them. Now, he had become their access to escape, and was providing for them. Jim was pondering the idea to hire him as a bodyguard until things shake out. He would first discuss it with his wife, knowing that it would seem like it came out of the blue, trusting a convict to protect their children.

They came across a rundown motel before they could finish eating. He was going to check them into two rooms beside each other. That couldn't be a hard

CHAPTER EIGHT

request considering the parking lot was empty. Before he got out of the car, there was a request from the First Lady who was doing a double take on the accommodations and rolling her eyes at Jim.

"Could you request fresh sheets and towels. I'll be happy to make the beds."

"Sure thing, you afraid of a little bed bug?"

She snapped back, "Yes, I am."

He came back with fresh linens, "Here you go, princess."

She smiled knowing that he didn't mean anything by his remark. But she and the girls would sleep better tonight knowing they were on fresh linens. They put the girls to bed and sat outside their door in some metal chairs overlooking the parking lot. They noticed George had left.

"He didn't leave us here, did he?"

"No, we have what he wants. He isn't going anywhere without us."

She turned to him and congratulated him on being able to grab the peanut butter lid. They were going to need that as proof that someone attempted to kill them, or at best, harm them. They sat in silence enjoying the cool breeze, but she knew that he was not at peace, there was turmoil going on in his head, and she didn't know if she should tap into that or let him figure things out on his own.

He finally commented on the events of the day and how they had unfolded.

"He was a trusted friend. The one who convinced me to run for office. We had such wonderful plans for this country. He deceived me." His heart was crushed.

"Honey, you could not have known his ultimate goal was to remove you, so that he could take the seat. He couldn't have gotten this far without you. You are the one that draws the crowds." She looked over at him and placed her hand on his cheek. "It's your captivating smile that warms the heart of the nation."

He placed his hand on hers and smiled that smile that melts her heart. "Thank you, I needed your encouragement."

"You've got all that I can give, but the one that can give you more, is the Lord. Emily told me in the car today that her angel was riding on the hood of the car."

"What? On the car?" You could see the shock in his face.

"Well, we agreed there was no room in the car." They both chuckled.

She pulled out a Bible, that she found in the motel room and was searching for a Scripture. She knew, she just didn't want to misquote it.

"Where did you find that?"

"It was in the drawer next to the bed. I figured we might could benefit from some of His Words being spoken over us tonight. Like Romans 8:31-39 (NIV), *'If God is for us, who can be against us? He who did not spare his own Son, but gave him up for us all—how will he not also, along with him, graciously give us all things? Who will bring any charge against those whom God has chosen? It is God who justifies. Who then is the one who condemns? No one. Christ Jesus who died—more than that, who was raised to life—is at the right hand of God and is also interceding for us. Who shall separate us from the love of Christ? Shall trouble or hardship or persecution or famine or nakedness or danger or sword? As it is written:*

'For your sake we face death all day long; we are considered as sheep to be slaughtered.'

No, in all these things we are more than conquerors through him who loved us. For I am convinced that neither death nor life, neither angels nor demons, neither the present nor the future, nor any powers, neither height nor depth, nor anything else in all creation, will be able to separate us from the love of God that is in Christ Jesus our Lord.'"

"You are so right. There is a lot in those verses that meet our needs. God is with us; we don't need to fear. My goodness, He sent an angel to ride along with us as we escaped danger. He is going to provide us with what we need. Which brings to mind something I wanted to talk to you about. What's your thoughts on hiring George as our bodyguard until we can shake the tree a bit and see who falls out?" He asked half expecting her to think he had lost his mind.

"Honestly, I think it's a good idea. We don't know who to trust. It doesn't seem that his intentions are to cause us any harm. He just went about getting our attention in an unethical way through an unconventional maneuver. In the days ahead we won't necessarily be together every step, and this way the girls and I can have some protection. I like that he thinks outside the box, a bit. It may rattle others that we are around."

"Good, it's what I was thinking too."

"And babe, remember the Word I just read, God has chosen you for this office, for this time. Jesus is interceding for us. We are conquerors. Nothing is going to get in the way of our future."

"You realize, we were focused on the wrong thing the whole time. The angels warning wasn't to just protect the girls, it was a warning for me, that there was a target on my back. Had I realized that earlier I would have removed myself from the family. I never meant to put you all in harm's way."

"We have always been in this together. We signed on with you, and we will see it through."

She flipped the Bible open to where someone else had marked a spot and was glancing over the words, when she stopped and told him he might want to hear what she was reading. Nodding as if he was interested, she began reading aloud Matthew 13:41-42 (NKJV).

"*'The Son of Man will send out His angels, and they will gather out of His kingdom all things that offend, and those who practice lawlessness, and will cast them into the furnace of fire. There will be wailing and gnashing of teeth. Then the righteous will shine forth as the sun in the kingdom of their Father. He who has ears to hear, let him hear!'*"

"Did you hear it? The righteous will shine forth, we will defeat our foes. We have angels present, possibly more than Emily's messenger angels. I believe we have warrior angels that will assist us in casting down this evil that has been perpetrated on us, as well as the nation."

"I pray you are right." He then corrected himself. "I know you are right. Target or not, we are going to come out on top. For we have the promises of God; He will rescue us, protect us, shelter us. He is our refuge, and no evil will touch us."

He was declaring truths over his family. And once something is decreed it is taken before the courts of heaven.

At that time George pulled up in front of his room.

"Where have you been?" Jim quizzed him.

"Look, I wanted to have a nice sit-down dinner. A man has got to eat. And I like real meat." Grinning big, he held up a bag. "I didn't forget you and your little lady."

He brought over a bag that had a steak and baked potato inside with a large salad. "I know the ladies like their salads."

"George, that was really nice of you." Jim smiled back at him, very appreciatively.

Nonchalantly adding, "I'll just add it to the tab I'm running."

"Speaking of that. What would you think of a job as a bodyguard for the family?"

He stopped and was caught off guard by the question. "Bodyguard?"

"You have kind of been doing that all day, looking out for the family and all. I just wanted to ask if you'd continue that work, after you get your lab results. Just for a while."

"Well, sure." He was tapping his foot in a nervous twitch kind of way. "I've never been somebody's bodyguard before, but I've had my buddies' backs in the joint. I guess that counts."

CHAPTER EIGHT

"Sure, it does." Jim thought it funny that he was trying to create a resume for the position.

Now that he had George's attention. "About the labs?"

"What about the labs? We are going in the morning." George wasn't wanting him to back out of the deal.

"Yes, but let's handle this slowly for Emily's sake. Let's first figure out if she is actually the Emily you are looking for. Then we can ask her what her thoughts are on whatever it is you are needing from her."

"She's mine, she looks just like her mother." There was no doubt in his mind that she was his daughter.

"One step at a time, George. Okay?"

"Sure, I'm not going to force anything. I know what that's like, and I don't want to do that to another." He was being agreeable.

"You want to talk about that?" He was giving him an opportunity to share a bit more about his circumstances.

"No." He was backing away and headed to his door. "I reaped what I sowed. Now, go on and eat that steak while it's still warm."

Chapter Nine

Answers

The President and First Lady shared with Emily the next morning about the labs. They repeated that it was her decision. They were not pushing her towards anything, and they were reassuring her that she would always be their daughter.

"I don't see the harm in seeking truth. Doesn't the Lord say that truth sets us free? I'm confident that whatever is discovered, I am always a child of God, and I am your daughter. It just might be that I am his as well."

They were both so proud of her and amazed at her maturity in handling what had been presented to her. They knocked on George's door to let him know that they were ready. No movement. They looked around the parking lot, no car. Where had he gone this time?

Suddenly the car came around the corner. George jumped out with a bag of biscuits and a big smile, along with a container holding three cups of coffee.

"Thought we should start out with a full tummy." He was looking straight at the girls, shaking the bag.

Jim smirked and thought, he is doing what we asked, watching out for the girls. They got in the car and ate their less than healthy breakfast.

George pointed out the water bottles in the back if they needed to wash the biscuits down. Excitement was written all over his face, he was going to find some answers he had been looking for. This may be the ticket to his healing.

They arrived at the lab and parked in the rear to avoid prying eyes. It was thought best that the First Lady and George take Emily inside, while the President sat in the car watching over the twins. The first thing was to determine paternity. Emily and George spit in a cup and gave a sample of hair to the technician, who told them to take a seat, it might take a while. George sat but his knees continued to shake up and down, as if he were getting a full workout. Emily sat calmly with her mother, noticing how nervous George was.

Emily looked over at George, put her hand on his knee, and said, "Don't worry, you will always be considered our hero."

"Hero?" He was puzzled by her comment, but she delivered it so sweetly and calmly that it did have a calming effect on him. "I'm nobody's hero, honey."

"But you are. You saved us from a dangerous situation. You put your life on the line to assist us."

"Yeah, but it's only because I was needing some answers."

"Maybe, maybe you were led there. You just didn't realize your full assignment."

He looked over at the First Lady shaking his head. He didn't know what to think of this little girl. But if she was his, he would be very proud to call her his daughter. About that time the technician walked out with the results. He stood before George and handed him the slip of paper.

"Congratulations, Papa." He said with a less than enthusiastic tone. He looked at the two adults and thought they made an odd couple but made no remarks.

CHAPTER NINE

George was ecstatic. He hugged Emily and looked into the eyes of the First Lady and saw concern. He was holding onto the piece of paper as if someone had handed him a golden ticket.

"I told you she was a spitting image of her mama."

The First Lady turned Emily towards her and explained that there was another test, now that the paternity test was resolved. It would require her to give some blood to determine if she was a match.

"A match? Didn't they just say he was my father?" She was confused.

"Yes, but not all family members are able to donate. God created us each uniquely and sometimes we are not compatible. Does that make sense? And are you willing to do this test?"

"George was willing to save us, so yes, I am willing to help him in return."

Her mom just grabbed her and held her tight with a tear in her eye. "You are so brave. I love you so much."

The technician took her by the hand, led her to another room and showed her where to take a seat. He gave her some juice and asked her if she wanted some crackers. She just shook her head. She might have been brave a minute ago, but she was feeling a bit scared now that she was separated from her mom, and she was looking at the equipment hanging around her.

She felt something brush across her hand and looked up. It was her angel standing beside her.

He didn't say anything, but she knew he was there to reassure her, everything was going to be all right.

Emily looked up at the angel and asked his name, realizing she had never asked him before. He usually came with a message for her to deliver. It was her assignment to listen carefully. The technician thought she was asking him what his name was, so he answered. Emily just smiled and nodded at him. The angel didn't speak at first, but then he did answer. She heard him say, Rex, in her head. She smiled even bigger in his direction realizing he was speaking to her without being heard by others.

The First Lady walked outside to let her husband and the girls know what was happening. She only took a moment and then darted back inside, checking to see if she could sit with Emily. She was told to wait outside the exam room, that it wouldn't be long, although the results would take a while. It was suggested that they go get some lunch and then come back. She wasn't about to leave Emily. Leaning against the wall, she felt something in her pocket. She had almost forgot; she handed the tech the inner lid from the peanut butter jar and asked if he could pull the trace of anything unusual from it. He thought it was an unusual request, but he would do what he could with it.

She sat down next to George. "I guess congratulations are in order."

"Thanks. Really thanks for everything. I don't know how things are supposed to work out, but I don't think I would have ever been able to get close to you all, if this had not happened this way."

She pondered what he said. It's true, with the tight security that is kept, it may have never happened. He may have never gotten to reveal who is daughter was.

"What's next, George? That is, if she isn't a match?"

"She's my last chance. There has not been a match found, among family or in the system."

"What's the odds of you surviving, whatever it is that you are fighting?"

"About the same as a fish out of water."

"Do you know the Lord Jesus Christ, as your Savior?"

"I've heard His name, but I don't know the man."

"He's no ordinary man, George, He is the Son of God. He came to save us from our sins, that carry us to the grave, an eternal darkness. He was sacrificed for our sins, that we may have eternal life and access to God the Father."

CHAPTER NINE

"I know that darkness you are talking about, I've lived hell on earth. I really don't want to live in hell for eternity. How do I live with this Jesus?"

"He is the key to the door that opens heaven for you. He has all the answers that you are looking for. You just need to accept Him as Lord of your life. Recognize your sinfulness, turn from your sinful lifestyle, and ask for forgiveness. See the truth, that He is the Son of God, He paid the penalty, the ransom for your sins, and took them to the grave, He was raised from the dead, to sit at the right hand of God the Father and rule from the throne of heaven."

"And here I thought your husband had power. Sounds like to me, Jesus has more authority."

"He does, He really does. Would you like me to lead you in prayer, to ask Jesus to come into your life?"

She was genuinely concerned for George. He may not get the results he was looking for, but she knew that Jesus would be the ultimate help that he needed.

"Yes ma'am, I need all the help I can get."

He was eager to accept help from anyone, and these people seemed to have some answers that he may need to carry on. He was focused on wanting to live.

"Father God, hear our prayers, George is ready to receive Jesus as Lord of his life as a gift from you. Make yourself real to him, Lord. We know that you will wash away his sins as if they were never his. That you will prepare him a place in heaven and welcome him home when it is his time to be received by you. In heaven Lord, you will wipe away every tear from his eyes, there will be no mourning, or crying, or pain, for you will make everything new. For you are faithful and true." She reached for George's hand. "Now, George do you receive Jesus Christ as your Lord and Savior?"

He was trying to hold it together, but he was sobbing, unsure of what had come over him. Through slow nods he managed to get out, "Yes."

"Confess your sin, ask for forgiveness, and ask Jesus to come into your heart as your Savior."

He paused, composed himself and then looked a little shocked.

"What's wrong?" The First Lady asked, confused as to why he hesitated.

"Well, my list is kind of long, miss. And it might take a while." He confessed.

"It's okay, you can just say sins, and fill in the blanks later as you repent and turn from those ways. I assure you that He knows all things." She was a bit amused by his candor and visualized him going through the list of his misdeeds.

He was good with that and promised the Lord he would get around to listing them all, as they came to him. The First Lady continued to share some points with him about how he may want to walk out his faith as a new Believer.

The First Lady handed him the Bible from the motel room. "I think you will be wanting to read a little more about your inheritance now. You are a part of the family."

George, not really being much of a reader, didn't know how to really handle a book. He flipped through the pages as if something was supposed to jump out at him. Landing at the back of the book and falling on some verses he wanted to ask about.

"Look here what this says in the back, this Revelation 21:5-8 (AMP), '*And He Who is seated on the throne said, See! I make all things new.*' That's just what you said ma'am. You said I was made new."

Something had come over him. He continued to read with enthusiasm, his heart was on fire. The Words he was reading seemed to ring true for him.

"'*Also He said, Record this, for these sayings are faithful (accurate, incorruptible, and trustworthy) and true (genuine). And He [further] said to me, It is done! I am the Alpha and the Omega, the Beginning and the End. To the thirsty I [Myself] will give water without price from the fountain (springs) of the water of Life. He who is victorious shall inherit all these things, and I will be God to him and he*

CHAPTER NINE

shall be My son. But as for the cowards and the ignoble and the contemptible and the cravenly lacking in courage and the cowardly submissive, and as for the unbelieving and faithless, and as for the depraved and defiled with abominations, and as for murderers and the lewd and adulterous and the practicers of magic arts and the idolaters (those who give supreme devotion to anyone or anything other than God) and all liars (those who knowingly convey untruth by word or deed)—[all of these shall have] their part in the lake that blazes with fire and brimstone. This is the second death.'"

He looked up at her with some peace. "I have to thank you, for saving me from that lake of fire. I haven't done all that's listed there, but I have done my share that would be displeasing."

"George, let me assure you that the Lord wants a relationship with you. I think He knew we would come to this point in time, and I would have an opportunity to share His Word with you. He has been chasing you and now He wants you to seek him. Take a look, in the Book at Psalm 139:5 (TPT)." Showing him how to find things.

George read aloud. "'*You've gone into my future to prepare the way.*'"

"Now skip down around to the verses 14-16." She suggested.

"'*How thoroughly you know me, Lord! You even formed every bone in my body when you created me in the secret place; carefully, skillfully, you shaped me from nothing to something. You saw who you created me to be before I became me!*'"

"He intimately knows you George, it's your turn to get to know Him." She stated.

"So, you are saying He knows all my flaws and still accepts me?" George was amazed.

"Yes, remember your sins are washed clean, He remembers them no more. God doesn't assess or judge us according to man's ways; His ways are higher than ours. He looks within. Even the most negative traits can be transformed into something positive, by the One who created you. Now look up

1 Peter 3:4. Flip towards the back of the book to find it." Again, pointing out how to find the chapter and verse, familiarizing him with the Bible.

She understood the importance of him seeing the Words for himself not just for her to be reading them out loud to him. This was his search for truth, for his life. Although she knew all too well Romans 10:17 (NIV), "*Faith comes from hearing the message, and the message is heard through the word about Christ.*" She just wanted him to be drawn to the Father as it states in Colossians, by spending time seeking truth for himself among the pages in the Bible. "*Giving thanks to the Father, Who has qualified and made us fit to share the portion which is the inheritance of the saints (God's holy people) in the Light. [The Father] has delivered and drawn us to Himself out of the control and the dominion of darkness and has transferred us into the kingdom of the Son of His love, In Whom we have our redemption through His blood, [which means] the forgiveness of our sins* (Colossians 1:12-14 AMP)."

George began to read slowly, emphasizing phrases, trying to take it all in as if he were digesting it. "'*Let it be the hidden person of the heart, with the incorruptible beauty of a gentle and quiet spirit, which is very precious in the sight of God (1 Peter 3:4 NKJV).*'"

The words were melting his heart as he sat rubbing the Bible wanting the message to sink in through his touch.

"He is looking at the attitude of the heart, integrity, kindness, gentleness. George, you have a good heart. We appreciate you; we see your heart; don't you think that God does? Allow the Word to speak to you. Things will fall into place when you turn to God for the answers."

The First Lady went on to share that if he would spend time with Jesus and come to know that he can trust Him, he would witness how God would change his circumstances, at least how he saw them. In other words, conforming his thoughts to Jesus's where He will be able to strengthen him during the trials of life. Jesus is the one that can shine light on his future steps.

CHAPTER NINE

This had been a very special day for George, even though the results did not come back as a match. He felt a certain freedom now. The fear of death had left him, although he may be facing it in the near future, he had Jesus on his side now. This brought him comfort. Looking for answers brought him to Jesus, at the same time reconnected him with his daughter, gave him a job to assist the First Family, and gave him a new hope.

His eyes fell upon Psalm 25 and he knew that it was his prayer.

"Make me know Your ways, O LORD; Teach me Your paths. Lead me in Your truth and teach me, For You are the god of my salvation; For you I wait all the day. Remember, O LORD, Your compassion and Your lovingkindnesses, For they have been from of old. Do not remember the sins of my youth or my transgressions; According to Your lovingkindness remember me, For Your goodness' sake, O LORD. Good and upright is the LORD; Therefore He instructs sinners in the way. He leads the humble in justice, And He teaches the humble His way. All the paths of the LORD are lovingkindness and truth To those who keep His covenant and His testimonies. For Your name's sake, O LORD, Pardon my iniquity, for it is great (Psalm 25:4-11 NASB)."

Song "I'm Going to Walk With Jesus" by Consumed By Fire

Chapter Ten

Confidence

It had gotten late; the twins were complaining about being hungry, again. The President knew that the twins had been very patient, they were obedient girls, but they were children after all, and they had limits. Their hunger had pushed those limits. He put on George's cap, when he arrived at the drive-through, he pulled the cap down low and avoided looking up at the cashier. The little cash that he remembered having wouldn't have gone very far, yet he had more than enough. He had simply reacted out of the girl's hunger and ordered without checking to see if he had the funds to cover the meal. His first thought was, the Lord does provide, and he also believed that God multiplies, especially now, based on what was just received. This was felt as if it was another supernatural occurrence.

There was an awareness of verses throughout the Bible that speaks to Gods ability to supply provision as well as multiply needs for His people. The stories of the water being turned to wine and the fact that it supplied the wedding needs, the baskets of fish and loaves feeding the five thousand, the oil that didn't run out for the widow. The Word is clear that He wants to provide for us, one verse that Jim loved to go to was Deuteronomy 28:12 (NKJV). "*The LORD will open to you His good treasure, the heavens, to give the rain to your land in its season, and to bless all the work of your hand. You shall lend to many nations, but you shall not borrow. And the LORD will make you the head and not the tail; you shall be above only, and not be beneath, if you heed the commandments of the LORD your God.*" Recognizing the goodness of God and His desire to pour out on His children can be seen also in Psalms 36:8 (NIV), "*They feast on the abundance of your house; you give them drink from your river of delights.*" And in Philippians 4:19 (NKJV) "*God shall supply all your need according to His riches in glory by Christ Jesus.*" God was supplying what they needed. His providential hand was on them, lunch was just a small sample of His provision and goodness.

These would be reasons why he continually lifts praise to God. Today was no different than any other day that he would thank God for His many ways that He has blessed his family. It had been taught to him at a very young age that lifting praise to God was out of respect, but there are many reasons to lift praise. God is holy and full of glory, His wisdom is unmatched, He is merciful and faithful, sure to fulfil His promises and keeps His covenants, He is powerful and fights our battles, defending us, delivering us, and saves us all out of love. Jim Patterson had confidence in God which increased other's ability to trust God.

As they waited on the food, he pondered on their situation a bit more and realized that decisions were needing to be made on how to proceed.

When they arrived back at the lab, the rest of the party was sitting at the back door of the facility, no worse for wear. George was smiling, his wife looked pleased, and Emily was happy to see her daddy. The results were in, they had what they needed from the lab.

CHAPTER TEN

They drove to a park that he had passed when he picked up lunch for all of them. There weren't many people out meandering on a weekday, and he felt there was enough coverage to shield them from prying eyes. It was declared time for the girls to have a little fun, so they were released to run and play on the playground, while he talked with his wife privately.

"I've had time to think, but I didn't want to make the decision without you, this involves all of us. I think it's best to head back to Washington, as soon as possible. We have evidence, and I need to catch him off guard before he sends more goons after us. I believe, if we head back, I can personally order more police and more security to surround us. He can't have infiltrated all agencies and everyone in them. If we have enough presence, there will be eyes, on those following us."

He looked deeply into his wife's eyes and asked what she thought of the idea.

"It's a good plan dear, and if we involve the media, there will be eyes on all of them as well, with plenty of cameras to catch them at any foul play."

"You're right, I hadn't thought of that. I'll make some calls and let some key people know we are coming back, except Allen, I want him in the dark where he belongs."

The calls were deliberately short, but the Capital police knew what to do, and his media contact knew to keep things on the downlow until they arrived. He would give them further information when things were set in place. This was promised to be a big story, one for the headlines. He knew he had the nation behind him, they were the ones who had elected him.

The President sat back down next to his wife, now a bit concerned, had he made the right decision. Where was the doubt coming from?

She stated, "You need to run with confidence."

"I'm running a bit shy in that area right now. Seems I have made some bad calls in the past."

"You must ask, in order to receive, Jim. Just like it says in John 16:23,24 (NKJV), *'Most assuredly, I say to you, whatever you ask the Father in My name He will give you. Until now you have asked nothing in My name. Ask and you will receive, that your joy may be full.'* Have you asked the Lord for help, for guidance, for wisdom like the angels have pointed out to us?"

"I guess I thought I had, I've read and focused on His Word, but I suppose I haven't actually asked for anything specific."

"You know that in Job 22:28 (NKJV) it states that *'You will also declare a thing. And it will be established for you; So light will shine on your ways.'* It's time you start declaring your path with confidence."

"I appreciate what you are trying to say, but. . ."

Stopping him in mid-stream, "I think you need some encouragement."

She looked around and spotted George watching over the girls. Moving over to where he was, she asked to borrow that Bible back for a moment. He had been reading it and watching the girls at the same time. The Holy Spirit was stirring in him, and he desired to know more about Jesus, now that they had been introduced. His time on this earth may be short, but he was going to make things right while he could. But he was happy to share the book with the First Lady. She came back over to her husband and opened to 1 Samuel 17 (NKJV).

"I think you will recall this story, but I want to point out this young man's confidence. He battled a giant with a single stone. All the men of Israel fled from this giant in fear, it states they were dreadfully afraid. They had to be bribed to fight him and still no one came forth, but this youth who had fought lions and bears to protect his flock was willing to step forward in faith. Listen to the confidence in his words spoken, starting here in verse thirty-six. *'Your servant has killed both lion and bear; and this uncircumcised Philistine will be like one of them, seeing he has defied the armies of the living God. Moreover, David* said, 'The LORD, who delivered me from the paw of the lion and from the paw of the bear, He will deliver me from the hand of this Philistine.' And Saul said to David, 'Go, and the LORD be with you!'"

She looked up at her husband. "Are you hearing the comparison honey, you have fought many battles in the corporate world and have always come out victorious, this battle with Allen seems immense, but not when you have God on your side. He has been looking out for you and us, through this entire attack. Now listen to the approach of David and be encouraged."

She looked back down at the pages and continued to read verse 1 Samuel 17:40,42 (NKJV). "'Then he took his staff in his hand; and he chose for himself five smooth stones from the brook, and put them in a shepherd's bag, in a pouch which he had, and his sling was in his hand. And he drew near to the Philistine. And when the Philistine looked about and saw David, he disdained him; for he was only a youth, ruddy and good-looking.' This is confirmation that your plan is good, the words there are 'he drew near.' Allen sees you as no threat, because he knows you are new to politics and to the ways of Washington. You are seen as a youth, with looks that got you in the office. You may be going into battle with less than fierce equipment, but you have something more powerful at your side."

He was seeing the point that his wife was making. Grasping her hand and smiling. "Yes, I do, I have you and I have God at my side."

She was looking in his direction and smiled as she continued to make her point. "I'll continue the Word in verse forty-five so that you might see how your plan will be delivered. The Lord is amazing, He is telling us exactly how this is going to play out. 'Then David said to the Philistine, 'You come to me with a sword, with a spear, and with a javelin, But I come to you in the name of the LORD of hosts, the God of the armies of Israel, whom you have defied. This day the LORD will deliver you into my hand, and I will strike you and take your head from you. And this day I will give the carcasses of the camp of the Philistines to the *birds of the air and the wild beasts of the earth, that all the earth may know that there is a God in Israel. Then all this assembly shall know that the LORD does not save with sword and spear; for the battle is the LORD's, and He will give you into our hands* (1 Samuel 17:45-47 NKJV).'"

She was fired up now. "Allen has defied y'all's plans, but he has also defied the plans that God has for this nation. You are to remove him from his high position as if taking his head off. Did you get that reference to '*the birds of the air and wild beasts of the earth*', that's the media. They will eat him alive. And you have a story to share with the nations on how God revealed things and protected us. I am almost giddy over that. Imagine the nations hearing our story, how the Gospel will be able to spread through the airways. Let's not forget that David hurried and ran toward the army with only a stone, he ran with confidence that the Lord was on his side and that he already had this battle won."

Jim had looked on as she read with such amazement as to how she applied the Word to their situation perfectly. Encouragement was rising in him, and the Holy Spirit was stirring him. He was fired up. They were well aware that the Bible is not meant to represent just one thing in time, its wisdom is for all time. One just needs to seek truth in the Word and allow it to be applied to their lives. Allow the Holy Spirit to guide them in truth and direction. The angel had told him to seek wisdom and his wise wife had found the encouragement her husband needed in the Word.

"Let's bring down that giant. And as the Word said, 'this day the Lord will deliver' him to us. I think it's a message we need to head back today. It may be getting late, but I would imagine the girls would love to sleep in their own beds tonight."

They spoke to George about coming to stay with them in the White House. It would give him the opportunity to get to know Emily better and

CHAPTER TEN

they could use someone they trusted to watch over the girls more closely. They insisted he could have a room right down the hall from the girls.

George responded, "So I've moved up in the world. From the Big House to the White House." They all laughed.

Then he got serious. "I appreciate you understanding that I want to get to know Emily. I don't believe I have a lot of time left. She was my last hope in finding a treatment plan. But I would have searched for her one way or another. So, this is a wonderful gift. Like I said before, if I had known she existed, I'd done everything in my power to take care of her. And now you are giving me that opportunity to prove that. Thank you."

He was genuine with his words, and it stirred emotions in all of them. George detected the downward mood and decided it was time to shake things up to change the atmosphere.

"Let's shake DC up a bit." He shouted.

He was shaking his fist in the air as an expression, let's go fight. Their battle was to begin. The President handed George a letter stating that he had special permission to be with the Presidential family as a bodyguard, and that he was allowed to carry a weapon, to protect them at all times. This was going to shake the establishment up, a felon carrying a weapon and hanging with the first Family.

"It's time to surprise a few people." The President stated smugly.

They all smiled and shouted, "Surprise."

The time had come to separate the sheep from the goats. It was agreed that all the agents couldn't be out to harm them, it had to be a few that had been infiltrated or bribed. Being in the public eye at this point might be safer than being in isolation, where anything could happen and be covered up. They controlled the narrative, now.

The President stated, "We are going home, and I am calling for a throw down."

It was time to battle. God's providential hand was on them, but God expects His people to step up and participate in carrying out His plans. Jim was to shoulder some of the weight, but to anticipate the move of God, the victory would be God's. He pondered the verses in Psalm 35 (NASB).

"*Contend, O LORD, with those who contend with me; Fight against those who fight against me. Take hold of buckler and shield And rise up for my help. Draw also the spear and the battle-axe to meet those who pursue me; Say to my soul, 'I am your salvation.' Let those be ashamed and dishonored who seek my life; Let those be turned back and humiliated who devise evil against me. Let them be like chaff before the wind, With the angel of the LORD driving them on. Let their way be dark and slippery, With the angel of the LORD pursuing them. For without cause they hid their net for me; Without cause they dug a pit for my soul. Let destruction come upon him unawares, And let the net which he hid catch himself; Into that very destruction let him fall* (Psalm 35:1-8 NASB)."

Jim couldn't overlook the number of things that were falling into place as if a master plan was coming together. He was confident that God was in control.

The girls were excited about going back home. They had been given the option to go to their grandparent's home for a visit, especially seeing how they were close enough now to their home, but they were ready to settle at home. They had been on the road and felt the wear and tear of the events that had taken place, it had been an emotional rollercoaster. They had been through a lot and needed assurances that they were safe. Being with their parents and being home would give them that comfort.

Song "Confidence" by Sanctus Real

Chapter Eleven

Angels

It had been a long late-night ride home, but it was worth it. The Capital police had met them at the front gates and secured the house for them. Jim had not forgotten what George had warned him of, the fact that security seemed lacking the night of the incident. George did his own surveillance before settling into the room down the hall from the girls. The girls crawled into their own beds, excited to be home. The President and First Lady wrestled with sleep, although they were both exhausted. The President was restless and anxious to confront his betrayer, knowing that he had early phone calls to make to put his plans in motion.

The house got quiet. Emily felt a little unnerved being in the same room where all the commotion started a few days earlier. She knew she would be watched over by her angels, but she kept looking at the balcony doors with the anticipation of trouble barging through. Although it had unfolded that it was her biological dad that had tried to enter, it was still a violation to her space and was making her feel unsettled. She was aware that there were extra guards posted all around the property and George was just down the hall. But she still felt she would sleep better if she was with the girls. The door creaked a little when she opened it. Another creak when she opened the girl's door and slipped inside. They popped up, surprised to see her. Apparently, no one was sleeping soundly.

"Would it be alright if I sleep with you guys tonight?"

"Sure, but it might be a tight fit." April giggled and looked down at the bed. Both girls were piled into a twin bed. Although the other twin bed sat empty, Emily had a plan.

"I've got an idea." Emily didn't falter.

She motioned for them to get out of the bed and help her push the two twin beds together. Now they could all sleep together across one big bed.

The First Lady had set the room up with twin canopy beds for the girl's arrival. Having read that twins like to be together, but it was important for them to establish their own identities and their own boundaries. So, she thought twin beds in the same room would fill that requirement. Although, she had not realized that April and June preferred sleeping together. Snuggling up on a twin bed didn't present a problem for them at all, they had slept that way all their life.

The girls were so pleased with themselves, they were unaware that they had caused quite the stir with all the furniture moving and the giggles filling the room, drifting down the hall.

Agents had shown up in the hallway to check on what was causing such a commotion. They found George already camped outside the girl's room. He was settled in for the night, leaned up against their door with a pillow, blanket, and a gun.

He had always been a light sleeper, which assisted him in watching after the girls. He heard the first creak of Emily's door and his feet hit the ground. As not to startle her, he just observed where she was going. It was obvious that she was a little nervous about sleeping by herself in the room that he had tried to enter. This now upset him, to know that he had caused her angst. All he could do now was to try and make things better for her, by watching over her.

The agents nodded at George and went on with their surveillance. It would be good to report in the morning, that they were on the job, and he witnessed their speed to the girl's room. This would comfort the First Lady.

The girls got their second wind, giggling and chatting in the big bed they had created. Emily admired the canopy over them. She had seen it in their room, but she had never slept under one.

"I like the canopy; it makes me feel secure." Emily commented.

"We love it. It feels like we are hidden under it." April stated.

"We were afraid to tell Mom we wanted one bed, the new one might not come with a canopy." April was shaking her head in agreement with what June was saying.

"Well, this works, you got the canopy and a big bed." They all giggled.

"Emily, were you afraid to be in your room?"

June asked the question that Emily was hoping wouldn't be asked. She really didn't know how to explain the feeling that came over her. And she didn't want to bring up bad memories of that evening that might frighten them.

"Not really afraid. I know my angels watch over me. I just felt funny in there, because of what happened before." She tried to keep it short.

"What are angels?" asked April.

"Where do they come from?" June asked.

Now this was going to get sticky. How much does she really tell them? Will it scare them or comfort them to know that angels watch over them and that they are really here with us? They had talked about angels before when April found the feather. Why didn't they question angels then? Does she reveal that she can see them? She pondered a lot before answering.

"Remember, I told you we have guardian angels that watch over us. Like when April found the feather. They were communicating with her that she would be all right."

"Yeah, I healed up really quick. So, my angel did that?"

"Possibly, they do provide aid, God says they are ministering spirits."

"Spirits? Like ghosts?" June asked astonished pulling the covers up closer.

"They aren't ghosts; not like you're thinking of. They are spirits, meaning you can't see them. They are heavenly beings that God created. He made them different from you and I."

"What does that mean?"

"It means they are from heaven. They have a different kind of body, it's spiritual, without weight, invisible to most. They exist on a level above matter, they aren't limited to our space. God created them for His purposes and uses them as His mouthpiece. They live with God in heaven, but they watch over us, as their assignment."

"Do they watch from heaven? Do they use telescopes?"

"Well actually, they can be with us. They watch us, they hang out with us, encouraging our walk with Jesus. They protect us and shield us from harm. And they give us messages from God."

"Ok, you just said a lot there. And I don't know that I understand it all. But I really don't understand the message part. How would they give messages to us if they are a spirit?"

"As I said, they are invisible to most, but Angels can be seen by some people." Oh, she knew she was treading in deep water now. This was going to be a long night.

"Who can see them? Someone you know?" April's eyes were big with curiosity.

CHAPTER ELEVEN

"Is it you, can you see angels?" June was a bit shocked by the concept of seeing an angel or that they exist around her. But Emily was speaking with authority as if she knew something that they didn't.

"Yes, I can see them when they want to be seen."

This caused the girls to get quiet. Emily could sense that they feared what she was saying, so she moved on quickly to explain a bit more.

"Look, angels are talked about in the Bible all over the place. You've heard the stories Mom has been reading to you. There are many instances where they were seen, talked to, and provided help to people. They didn't show up on the pages of the Bible and then disappear. They are still here among us and working for the Lord."

This got their attention and got them thinking. But they were not the only ones listening to what was being said. George was on the other side of the door taking in all that was said. He was surprised that his daughter was seeing angels. Accepting Jesus in his life was a new journey for him, but now he was processing his daughter's gifts.

She went on to say, "Who shut the mouths of the lions? An angel sent by God. Who told Hagar to go back to Sarah? Yes, an angel. Who spoke to Mary? An angel of the Lord. Who freed Peter from jail? An angel. Do you remember the Hebrew verse 13:2 (NIV), *'Do not forget to show hospitality to strangers, for by so doing some people have shown hospitality to angels without knowing it.'*"

The girls shook their heads. They had not known much about the Bible except what their mom had taught them. Emily was lucky enough to have studied the Bible, so she knew about the Scriptures. It dawned on her that the angels had something to do with that. Surely, they had shown her that Scripture along the way. Emily continued to share another verse with them from Colossians 1:16 (NASB).

"Paul, one of Jesus' leaders, wrote, '*For by Him all things were created, both in the heavens and on earth, visible and invisible, whether thrones or dominions or rulers or authorities---all things have been created through Him and for Him.*' For Him, that's Jesus, he created all things for the pleasure and purposes of God. This is why we praise God for all things because He is so good. I believe that God knew we would be weak and at times we would need help, so He created angels to watch over us, to be there when we needed aid. They were there for me many times when I was in the System."

"How do you know when they are with you?" Their curiosity was heightened as they huddled together for comfort.

"You don't always see them, but you might feel their presence. Kinda like animals sense other animals being around, it's just instinct or perception. Other times they make themselves known. The Bible has even talked about them showing up in human form."

"Do you think George is an angel?" April was inquisitive, she realized he had shown up when then needed his help.

"No, he is my father. But you are correct in saying that he came at a good time."

"I'm going to have to start reading the Bible, sounds like there is a lot of good stories in there." June drug out her picture book Bible from her bedside and started to flip through the pages. Realizing that there were more pictures than words, like the one Emily used.

"They seem like stories, but they are our history. And you won't find all this information in that picture book. You have to read the real Book to get all the facts."

"You said you see them. How come we don't see them?"

"It's a gift I guess, I have heard that it's called being a seer. There is a great story about a famous seer in the Bible found in Numbers, where the donkey could see the angel, when the seer couldn't."

CHAPTER ELEVEN

The girls thought this was funny and started laughing under the sheets. Then more questions popped in their heads. "How did they know the donkey could see the angel?"

"At first it was its strange behavior, then the donkey talked."

More laugher ensued, the thought of a donkey talking was hilarious. Jane insisted she was going to read that story in the morning.

"There are other demonstrations in the Bible that you would find interesting as well. For instance, Elisha's servant was upset about a trap that had been set for them. But Elisha wasn't upset because he knew the protection that was provided around them. He could see something that his servant couldn't see. He asked the Lord to open his servant's eyes, so that he could see what was all around them."

The girls were excited, "What did he see?"

"God's Host of angels, with chariots of fire."

"Cool, they ride on chariots of fire, I guess they were lightning fast."

"Did they go to battle?"

"Not in this story, it was to instill confidence in Elisha and his companion. To persuade them that the strength of an enemy army is never an actual threat when you're on God's side. But Elisha did win. You can read about it tomorrow in 2 Kings, Chapter 6, I believe.

"You said that Elisha asked the Lord to open the servants' eyes to see the angels. Have you ever asked the Lord to open someone's eyes to see what you can see?"

"No. It actually has never occurred to me to do that."

"How many angels are there?" April was curious and kept looking around the room as if her eyes were suddenly going to see angels in the room with them.

"Well, we all have guardian angels, so that means there is a lot of them, there are a lot of us. Rex, one of my angels, told me once that it's a great multitude of them, and I remember reading in Matthew 26:53 (NASB) that Jesus could have called on them to rescue Him. But He didn't, because He had an assignment to save us. It read something like, '*Do you think that I cannot appear to My Father, and He will at once put at My disposal more than twelve legions of angels?*'"

"What's a legion?"

"Rex told me that a legion could be six thousand men, and if you multiplied that by twelve, then you'd have somewhere around 144,000 angels. You could say that Jesus had a lot of bodyguards. Can you imagine Dad having that many bodyguards around?"

"We'd never be able to move around."

"Yeah, it's crowded enough as it is." June rolled her eyes.

Emily continued. "God's throne is surrounded by angels, I've read in Revelation 5 that there were thousands upon thousands, and ten thousand times ten thousand. So, I don't think we can put an exact number on them."

"Emily, how do you remember all those facts?" April's curiosity was piqued once again. It was troublesome for her to remember history facts for a test.

"I was gifted with a photographic memory, which means I don't forget much."

"I bet school is easy for you." April was wishing she had some of that gift.

"Hey, those angels in the story were going to fight a battle to help that man. Would they fight for us?" June was now thinking of their circumstances and hoping for things to go well for her dad.

"Angels do fight battles for us." Emily replied.

"Will they fight Dad's battle?" She wanted a direct answer regarding their circumstances.

"I would imagine Dad has angels battling for him, and with him. Because I know that he has had messages from God."

"How do you know that?"

"Because I delivered the messages."

CHAPTER ELEVEN

"Are you an angel?" The twin's eyes got big.

"No. I'm your sister. But I have been given assignments, to deliver messages from the angels, that come from God."

"So, let me get this right. God sends a message through the angel, and gives it to you, so that you can deliver it to the person that it's for?"

"Yes."

"Wow! How long have you been doing that?"

"A long time."

"Emily, you aren't that old, how long could it actually be?"

"I guess it started when I was around four. It just seems like my whole life. I have always been able to see the angels. I just didn't know exactly what I was seeing at first. They were there watching me, sometimes playing with me, when I was alone. And when I was scared, they comforted me. There were times that they protected me from harm."

"What do you mean?"

"I don't want to go into it. But I imagine you found yourselves in difficult situations going through the System?"

"Yes, I guess so, we had some harsh homes that we were in, but we really didn't know any different, until we came here and saw what a family is really like."

"Yeah, we were made to do a lot of work. We didn't have a lot to eat. We were always the last to be fed; leftovers had a different meaning for us. We never had a room of our own, like we do now. There were bunk beds lining the walls. I guess that's why we are so used to sleeping together in a twin bed. It's what we know."

"I'm glad you didn't experience any physical abuse."

"Did you?" They looked concerned and heartbroken at the thought. This was a lot of information for them to comprehend.

"There were many attempts, but my angels always protected me." Emily stated pensively not wanting to reveal all that she had endured. There was no need to upset the twins, it was best to leave them with a comforting outlook of things.

"Let's pray for Dad's protection and any help that the angels could offer would be greatly appreciated."

They stopped and prayed together as they were taught. Don't just say you're going to pray for someone, stop and do it right then. It was very late; the sun was about to surface, and they were just bedding down. It was going to make for a long and slow day ahead.

George had overheard all that was shared through the night hours. He was offering prayers too. He thanked the angels for watching over his daughter and keeping her from harm. The thought that she had experienced such danger broke his heart. He was also giving thanks to the Lord for his salvation, and for the opportunity to meet his daughter, and now to discover more about his daughter. She was not only a beautiful child, but she was also gifted. It had been revealed to him tonight, that she had a photographic memory, that she spoke to angels and actually had an assignment from God to deliver messages to people. He was feeling blessed to know about these things and given the opportunity to watch over her.

Song "Speak to the Mountains" by Chris McClarney

Chapter Twelve

Twisted Agenda

The President had the evidence he needed; it was time to face where he thought the threat had originated from and why. He had gotten up very early to confront the one behind the threats. It was hard to believe that such a close friend could betray him at this level. He wanted to hear it directly from his mouth. What kind of reason could he give for treason?

Jim and Allen had worked so closely on their agenda for the country. Grand plans were put in place to turn things around and help people see how they needed to follow godly directives to have a prosperous nation. They wanted to remind people that God was the one who had inspired the Constitution, giving the people liberty and freedoms from tyranny. If they continued down the path they were on, they would be headed for a socialistic regime, or worse communism, where they would lose their freedoms and their voice to tyranny and dictatorship.

A sense of false prosperity and time had fostered laziness in the people. They had winked at disobedience to the Lord, resulting in the condition of the country they were living in. Complacency had been proven to have crippled the nation. They no longer took the time to research and seek out God fearing people to lead them. They had forgotten that their vote was their voice, and it should have been taken seriously. Without properly vetting people running for office, they ended up with those in a race that promoted themselves, not an agenda for their constituents. They were motivated by prestige, power, and financial gain, and even worse they had been persuaded to follow a globalist agenda. They did not have hearts of servanthood, they had the mindset of the hood, stealing from the people to advance themselves and their evil projections, exploiting the people had become a way of life.

The Scripture that came to mind for Jim and Allen at the time was, 1 Kings 14:22-24 (NKJV), *"Now Judah did evil in the sight of the LORD, and they provoked Him to jealousy with their sins which they committed, more than all that their fathers had done. For they also build for themselves high places, sacred pillars, and wooden images on every high hill and under every green tree. And there were also perverted persons in the land. They did according to all the abominations of the nations which the LORD had cast out before the children of Israel."*

It was going to take another revival to fully awaken the people as to how bad things had gotten. Allen and Jim were wanting to spearhead such an event. A revival marks a time when the Lord invades a community, reviving its saints and calls the sinner to repentance. Jim had studied revivals and their effects in different locations, how they moved whole communities towards God. His desire was to stir something within the entire nation.

He discovered historical facts as in the American colonies during 1730's through 1740's, where people were impacted by the concept that religion had grown stale and had become complacent, during a time when the nation was exploring the frontier and moving farther away from churches and morals. The Great Awakening with Jonathan Edwards and George Whitefield came with a message to awaken Christian faith and return to a religion that was relevant to the people of the day. They spoke of being born into sin, the need to connect with God by asking for forgiveness and called them to work on a personal relationship with God. The Second Great Awakening was less emotionally charged, yet it led to the founding of colleges and seminaries. Religion was reinvigorated during this time, with a desire for a godly nation. They reached a younger generation who had lacked a relationship with Jesus. Drawing them in with the emphasis of being a new creation in Christ, which led them to share their revelation with the older generation, therefore the message was spread. Such movements changed entire towns. This is what Jim wanted to flourish across the country. They were still working on ways to reach the multitudes in varying generations, learning what captured their attention so that it would take root.

Jim was reflecting on what he had heard about Cane Ridge Revival, which occurred in 1801. Where over 25,000 gathered in the fields of Kentucky to hear ministers preaching from a stump. Cries of mercy were heard from people being convicted by the message, to then what turned to praises of Precious Jesus, being shouted. Voices were amplified by a supernatural force getting their attention and resulting with many coming to Jesus. There was an explosion of church plantings to followed. How could they do that again? Jim was very aware that Jesus was on his side, could he not orchestrate another movement, something similar to this or the one that he heard about in California.

The Azusa Street, California Revival of 1906 was a renowned three-year spiritual experience, where people fell under the power of the Holy Ghost. People were stirred to speak in tongues and healings occurred, something that couldn't be overlooked. The whole city was stirred by the activities of the Lord. He could imagine a whole nation being stirred like that.

The verse that kept ringing in Jim's mind was Psalm 77:11,12 (NKJV), *"I will remember the works of the LORD; Surely I will remember Your wonders of old. I will also mediate on all Your work, and talk of Your deeds."* Does the Bible not tell us to earnestly remember in several Scriptures? How can people so easily forget the move of God?

Each revival was building on what was done before. If they could tap into what was happening during those events in time, then they could move onto something greater for the nation and for God's kingdom. Transforming a nation, one community at a time, is what he had in mind. He was reminded of Jesus' Words in Matthew 28:18-20 (NKJV), *"All authority has been given to Me in heaven and on earth. Go therefore and make disciples of all the nations, baptizing them in the name of the Father and of the Son and of the Holy Spirit, teaching them to observe all things that I have commanded you; and lo, I am with you always, even to the end of the age."*

Reform needed to come to the nations. Teach them principals and the commands of God, infiltrating all areas of society so that influence comes from the top, resulting in bringing them to Jesus. This enlightenment transforms how one thinks, therefore taking the country in a new direction. If a country could be led by Godly principals, then the land would be blessed by God. His administration knew this was their goal.

Government and systems of society had been taken over by people with evil agendas. Leaders were motivated by power and overwhelming greed, not serving their constituents as they were elected to do. They had been leaving behind conservative ideology and embracing socialism, what seemed like elitism, putting themselves over others. There had been attacks on the Constitution, which results in attacks on individual freedoms. Things had gotten so bad that people were having to sue the government for overstepping their boundaries, versus the government working for and serving the people. Many witnessed what was clearly a two-tier system of justice. They were wanting to dislodge evil and free the nation, returning it to a just nation under God. They didn't want to be bystanders anymore.

CHAPTER TWELVE

Allen had cited Philippians 2:4 (NKJV), *"Let each of you look out not only for his own interests, but also for the interest of others."* He had driven home the point that they had both been successful men, it had become time for them to give back and share with the nation what they had to offer. It was agreed that Philippians 2:13-15 (NKJV) spoke to them. *"For it is God who works in you both to will and to do for His good pleasure. Do all things without complaining and disputing, that you may become blameless and harmless, children of God without fault in the midst of a crooked and perverse generation, among whom you shine as lights in the world."*

It had been stated that they had a calling on their lives, and they needed to follow through with their assignment that they felt was from God. It was bigger than them. Their assignment was spiritual as much as it was physical. It was their time to shine. They were going to shake things up in Washington and throughout the land. Shake them until the corruption was sifted out.

He recalled the Scripture they shared with each other from Hebrews 12:25-29 (NKJV). *"See that you do not refuse Him who speaks. For if they did not escape who refused Him who spoke on earth, much more shall we not escape if we turn away from Him who speaks from heaven, whose voice then shook the earth; but now He has promised saying 'Yet once more I shake not only the earth, but also heaven.' Now this, 'Yet once more,' indicates the removal of those things that are being shaken, as of things that are made, that the things which cannot be shaken may remain. Therefore, since we are receiving a kingdom which cannot be shaken, let us have grace, by which we may serve God acceptably with reverence and godly fear, For our God is a consuming fire."*

Allen and Jim had planned to educate society on the Founding Fathers principles and the history of the country. Leading them back to Biblical foundations. It would be a job to cleanse the corruption that had infiltrated the leadership in Washington, that had become so stagnant. Yet, they had stirred the people to action, and actions were creating changes. A shattering of the establishment had begun with their election. They were the ones on fire.

There had been strong structural changes happening in the economy. They had lowered tax burdens, applied regulation cuts so that businesses could boom, created energy dominance, and brought back manufacturing to the States where it belonged. The military had been revamped and built up, versus being underfunded and underequipped. They were securing the border for the security of the nation, while implementing changes in the emigration laws, so that it was a faster, more efficient system. The nation was thriving, and the people were happy, they felt safe once again.

His administration was promoting faith which secures the family unit, working at securing and cleaning up the streets, which allows for business to expand and society to flourish. The big agenda that was on the table now was redesigning the monetary system. It was time for a change. The country was destined for something great, and they were there to help her on her way.

As Jim reflected on his beginnings as President, on his accomplishments, and on the events of the day, he was now concerned about other members in his cabinet. Who else is giving me bad counsel, working to stab me in the back? What kind of twisted agenda have they come up with? Were they all betraying me? Or more importantly, the people of this nation. He realized he had been deceived, and he was going to get to the bottom of it, they will be shamed publicly for the sin that they have committed on the nation, it was an attempt to destroy the country from within.

He was reminded of the Scripture from Hosea 4:6-9 (AMP), "*My people are destroyed for lack of knowledge; because you [the priestly nation] have rejected knowledge, I will also reject you that you shall be no priest to Me; seeing you have forgotten the law of your God, I will also forget your children. The more they increased and multiplied [in prosperity and power], the more they sinned against Me; I will change their glory into shame. They feed on the sin of My people and set their heart on their iniquity. And it shall be: Like people, like priest; I will punish them for their ways and repay them for their doings."*

King Solomon came to mind, how he had found favor with God, who had blessed him and yet Solomon's heart turned over time, he became too ambitious. Had this happened to Allen? All of his achievements would be lost along with his legacy, just like King Solomon. He became prideful and turned to idolatry. Yes, pride has taken hold of Allen, and he is about to see his own destruction. He hammered down on Proverbs 16:18 (NIV84). *"Pride goes before destruction, a haughty spirit before a fall."*

The weight of the world seemed to be on Jim's shoulders, betrayal always hits the heart in a hard way. God's message warned him to guard his heart, His Word was clear about difficult days that will come, and how one was to avoid such people. That meant harm. He will have to look closely at the people he brings into his inner circle and discern who is trustworthy. His thoughts went to 2 Timothy 3:1-5 (NASB), where he now recognized many of Allen's hidden characteristics. *"But realize this, that in the last days difficult times will come. For men will be lovers of self, lovers of money, boastful, arrogant, revilers, disobedient to parents, ungrateful, unholy, unloving, irreconcilable, malicious gossips, without self-control, brutal, haters of good, treacherous, reckless, conceited, lovers of pleasure rather than lovers of God, holding to a form of godliness, although they have denied its power; Avoid such men as these."*

It distressed Jim a great deal that he had not noticed the change in Allen. Reflecting now, on the story of David, when his own men had wanted to stone him because their hearts were grieved. Yet David was strengthened after inquiring from the Lord what he should do. *"Shall I pursue this troop? Shall I overtake them?" And He answered him, "Pursue, for you shall surely overtake them and without fail recover all* (1 Samuel 30:8 NKJV)." Jim found strength in those words when all seems lost, turn to God, and pursue truth. The Word states that he will recover all. That's what he was going to rely on.

His heart shouted Psalm 59:1,2 (NKJV) with each pounding heartbeat, as a war drum. *"Deliver me from my enemies, O my God; Defend me from those who rise up against me. Deliver me from the workers of iniquity, And save me from bloodthirsty men."* Reminded once more, *"For with God nothing will be impossible* (Luke 1:37 NKJV)."

Having risen early, reading his Bible in preparation for the battle ahead of him and looking for more assurances from the Lord. He knew he would find answers in the Bible. The angels' directives had been to keep his eyes on the Word.

Sure enough, he found what he was seeking when he came across Psalm 7:6-11 (NASB). *"Arise, O LORD, in Your anger; Lift up Yourself against the rage of my adversaries, And arouse Yourself for me; You have appointed judgment. Let the assembly of the peoples encompass You, And over them return on high. The LORD judges the people; Vindicate me, O LORD, according to my righteousness and my integrity that is in me. O let the evil of the wicked come to an end, but establish the righteous; For the righteous God tries the hearts and minds. My shield is with God, Who saves the upright in heart. God is a righteous judge, And a God who has indignation every day."*

"Behold, he travails with wickedness, And he conceives mischief and brings forth falsehood. He has dug a pit and hollowed it out, And has fallen into the hole which he made. His mischief will return upon his own head, And his violence will descend upon his own pate (Psalm 7:14-16 NASB)."

It was time to turn the tables on them. It was time to surprise Allen and allow him to dig his own pit. He has birthed his own trouble with me and with the Lord. He will see all his achievements turn to dust.

He arrived at Allen's office even before his staff, but he was not alone. The Capitol police were strategically placed as to not create an awareness until the proper time. The selected media was informed to stand down until the

CHAPTER TWELVE

commotion started. If they handled it properly, they would get a headline from the President himself.

Allen walked in his office and Jim was sitting in his seat. It caught him off guard, he stopped in his tracks, blinked as if he couldn't believe what he saw, and then quickly shut the door behind him.

"Jim, Mr. President, what are you doing here?" He was definitely flustered.

"Did I surprise you?" Jim was calm, yet eager to get to the truth.

"Why yes, you did. How did you get here? I thought you were still in hiding?" He questioned more calmly now. Wondering why there had been no report.

"No, I thought better of that plan. Thought it might be best to be among many eyes watching my moves and my family's moves."

"What do you mean, Jim? Were my men not taking care of you?" He was fishing.

"No, in fact we felt threatened by them. You want to explain why that is, Allen?"

"I don't know what you are talking about?"

"Okay, let me lay it on the table, literally." He pulled out the peanut butter lid and the results from the lab and laid it on Allen's desk.

Allen's eyes got big, and you could see the wheels turning in his head. "What is that?"

"It's lab results. You tried to poison my kids, Allen?" Jim's face was turning red with anger, but he was trying to stay in control. What he really wanted to do was to leap across the desk and strangle him.

"I don't know what you are talking about." Trying denial as his tactic.

Allen was looking scared, giving himself away. It was confirmation to Jim as to what was going on. The angel's messages had been correct, he had been betrayed by a brother.

"How could you have fallen so far? We are like brothers, and you betrayed me. But Allen, you not only betrayed me, but you also betrayed the people of this nation. You took an oath of office and you tried to assassinate the rightful President of the nation. That is treason."

"It's not me, I don't know who tried to do this to you. On my honor, I don't know anything."

"Man up, Allen, you've lost my trust, and you have no honor. It's apparent that all men have a price. No matter what they have to lose. You've lost everything, your position, your character, trust, your achievements, and yes, your honor. You will be shamed in front of the world. That is all I can do for you. The Lord, however, may look upon things differently. He will judge you in His own way. His gavel will come down hard on you. It's His plans that you have tried to destroy."

"I have not destroyed anyone's plans. You must believe me." Begging wasn't working, nor did it look good for a grown man.

"That's just it, I don't. We answered a calling together, to lead this country back to the Lord. To put this nation back on track and to be prosperous again. We proved we could do it in less than one term. I don't understand why you decided to jump the tracks. We were getting things accomplished. You know that without a good foundation there will be collapse. We have the people headed in God's direction, where He wants them."

Jim was practically moaning over his disgust and disappointment. He knew how far they had come bringing stability to a nation that was in turmoil. They couldn't recognize good from evil. They had drifted from all the fundamentals of faith: recognizing God as creator of all things, that gender was male and female, marriage was between man and a woman, the sanctity of life at conception, the virgin birth, and Jesus as the Son of God. This attempt on his life and his family's life was going to bring a setback to the nation, in how people perceived what they had been telling them. They will question the good that has been established. They will question if leadership ever had an authentic relationship with Jesus.

"Why have you provoked God this way? *'Is there no balm in Gilead? Is there no physician there? Why then is there no healing for the wound of my people* (Jeremiah 8:22 NIV)?' We were that balm, Allen, we were elected to save them from a disastrous fate. We were to heal the nation. We were the ones defeating the foes of our country. If the nation falls it will be because of your judgment that has been cast on them like a shadow. *'The nations will hear of your shame; your cries will fill the earth. One warrior will stumble over another; both will fall down together* (Jeremiah 46:12 NIV).' I for one, am not going down with you."

"I understand you are upset. I'd be upset too if I thought I was betrayed. But I'm not that man. I haven't betrayed you." He was still squirming.

"Allen, I'll give you that, you can be very convincing." He almost laughed. "But you aren't that man I believed had my back. I was depending on you for help. When God was telling me to use my own discretion to work things out. Then you go using God's Word on me and telling me not to be afraid. When the whole time you had a target on my back."

He paused a minute and continued to say, "Well you were right about one thing the Lord has been with us the whole time. And I think you should heed Jeremiah's message, because you used God's Word falsely to me and to the people of this nation. By attaching your name with His, you led people astray. You have corrupted our agenda, God's agenda."

He opened the Bible to Jeremiah 23:24,26,27,32,39,40 (NASB), and began reading.

"*'Can a man hide himself in hiding places so I do not see him?' declares the LORD. 'Do I not fill the heavens and the earth?' declares the LORD. 'How long? Is there anything in the hearts of the prophets who prophesy falsehood, even these prophets of the deception of their own heart, who intend to make My people forget*

My name by their dreams which they relate to one another, just as their fathers forgot My name because of Baal? Behold, I am against those who have prophesied false dreams, declares the LORD. And related them and led My people astray by their falsehoods and reckless boasting; yet I did not send them or command them, nor do they furnish this people the slightest benefit, declares the LORD. Therefore, behold, I will surely forget you and cast you away from My presence, along with the city which I gave you and your fathers. I will put an everlasting reproach on you and an everlasting humiliation which will not be forgotten.'"

Allen was getting worried as if judgment was going to fall on him any moment. His face and body language gave way to stress.

"You rode my coattails all the way to the White House. But that wasn't enough for you, you wanted my seat. And I was the only way you were going to get there. Does that sound about right, Allen?"

Allen was getting inflamed now, Jim was starting to push the right buttons.

"You would have never made it here, if it wasn't for me." Allen spewed the words with such rage, his eyes looked as if he was sending fiery darts at Jim.

"Oh, I think it's the other way around, friend." The Scripture came back to Jim's mind that the angels had delivered, *'adversaries will not be able to contradict or resist* (Luke 21:15 NKJV)'. He chuckled to himself; God is good.

Then God laid on Jim's heart Psalm 140:1-3 (NKJV). He stared down Allen as he spoke, as if delivering a sermon with fire.

"*'Deliver me, O LORD, from evil men; Preserve me from violent men, Who plan evil things in their hearts; They continually gather together for war. They sharpen their tongues like a serpent; The poison of asps is under their lips.'* That poison was delivered to our door."

He looked down at the lab results and back at Allen. "You intended harm on my family. Remember how we said the children are our future, why would you want to harm my children? Can you explain that?"

CHAPTER TWELVE

Allen answered smugly revealing some truths. "If they got sick enough, you would have to go to a hospital, things happen in a hospital, Jim. Things that can easily be covered up."

"So now, you are going to fess up?" Jim glared at Allen.

"You have no proof I've done wrong." Smugly remarking, thinking he had covered all his tracks.

Jim shook his head confidently, piercing his heart with his determined look.

"Look, Allen I don't begin to understand your twisted agenda, but I know who I put my trust in."

Then he cited Psalm 27:1-3 (NKJV) throwing Allen under the bus. "'*The LORD is my light and my salvation; Whom shall I fear? The LORD is the strength of my life; Of whom shall I be afraid? When the wicked came against me to eat up my flesh, My enemies and foes, they stumbled and fell. Though an army may encamp against me, my heart shall not fear; though war may rise against me, in this I will be confident.*' I am confident in the Lord, and He has given me what I need to prove you are guilty, without you confessing to me. But I now have that on tape as well."

"You've recorded all this?" He was shocked and waiting for the hammer to fall.

"Allen, do you see me as a fool? I not only have you recorded here, but I have the phone that you gave to your rouge hired help, a witness that overheard your instructions, along with the evidence from the lab. It will be better for you if you cooperate and give up who else is involved. I know you didn't spearhead this all by yourself."

Jim paused a minute then quoted Proverbs 3:35 (NKJV) confidently. "'*The wise shall inherit glory, But shame shall be the legacy of fools.*'"

At that moment the Capital police came in and surrounded Allen. Proverbs 3 was their trigger phrase. He was handcuffed and hauled off in shame through the building. When he got outside, the media had cameras filming the whole thing. The buzzards were swarming, they would eat this deception up until every morsel was exposed. This event would be in the headlines by the afternoon and talked about around the world.

Jim had wished Allen could have come up with an excuse of blackmail, threats, or some huge payoff, but it was all for power. He had opened the door to pride and to Satan, allowing him to be coerced. Vice President wasn't enough, he was convinced he could have the ultimate seat of power, if he just removed his good friend. At what point had Allen actually hatched this deception was unknown, but Jim felt that it had been fueled once they had moved to the corrupted city of DC.

The verses that were ringing true in his head were Isaiah 41:9-13 (NKJV). "*You whom I have taken from the ends of the earth, And called from its farthest regions. And said to you, 'You are My servant, I have chosen you and have not cast you away: Fear not, for I am with you; Be not dismayed, for I am your God. I will strengthen you, Yes I will help you, I will uphold you with My righteous right hand.'*

Behold, all those who were incensed against you Shall be ashamed and disgraced; They shall be as nothing, And those who strive with you shall perish. You shall seek them and not find them-- Those who contended with you. Those who war against you Shall be as nothing, As a nonexistent thing. For I, the LORD your God, will hold your right hand, Saying to you, 'Fear not, I will help you.'"

"Me On Your Mind" by Matthew West

Chapter Thirteen

Morning Chat

The morning had come early for Jim, who had already engaged in his very important agenda, while the rest of the family slumbered in the comfort of their home. When the First Lady woke, she came walking down the hall to check on the girls. She saw George sitting at the twin's bedroom door. Wondering what had happened to warrant him sleeping at the door. Her pace quickened, and George stirred. He hopped up as if he had done something wrong when he saw her face.

She shook her head, confused by the scene. "Are the girls alright?"

"Oh yes, they're fine. They had a long night of giggling and talking." Trying to reassure her.

"I thought they were tired. I know I was."

"They got their second wind rather early in the evening."

"Well, I'll check in on Emily." She started down the hall when George cleared his throat and pointed to the twin's room.

"She got spooked a bit and joined them last night."

"Well, that had to be interesting with twin beds."

"They are clever girls."

"Oh really, maybe I should poke my head in there."

"I'd give them a little more time ma'am; they just went to sleep at sunup."

"Oh my. Well, maybe you'd like to join me for a cup of coffee this morning. I think you have a lot to share with me. Jim headed out quite early this morning. It will be just the two of us."

"Sure, I'll have a cup. I'm pretty good in the kitchen too. You want me to whip up some breakfast?" Wanting to be of assistance to her.

"I'll start with coffee, thank you. Maybe the girls would like some breakfast when they get up."

Walking into the kitchen she released the kitchen staff and let them know that they would be fine on their own this morning. The staff looked confused but figured she was wanting some privacy with the new staff member.

While pouring two cups of coffee she asked George, "If there was something she needed to know about what took place last night?"

George responded humbly. "Well, like I said, Emily got a bit spooked about the balcony. I'm afraid that is all on me. And I will do all I can to help her feel safe again."

He paused and took a sip of coffee; it was obvious he was remorseful for what he had done and for the emotional effect it had on his daughter.

The First Lady came up with a solution to help the situation as quick as she sat down.

"We will have security bars installed at the balcony doors right away. That should have been done before we moved in here, anyway. This has just taught us to rethink some safety issues."

She wasn't upset about the event George was involved in anymore. They had all come to love George and wanted to help him. She was particularly fond of him because she had been able to bring him to Jesus, and now, she just wanted to encourage his walk with Jesus.

"I'm glad she found refuge in the twin's room, but it's beyond me how they all found a place to sleep."

"Oh, that's the other thing. They moved the furniture around to create a bigger bed. Apparently, the twins sleep together in one twin bed anyway. I'm not sure why Emily just didn't sleep in the other twin bed. But they wanted to be all together."

"Well, that explains why one bed is always made up. I just thought one of them was super neat and made the bed when she got up in the morning. Not exactly something a mother would complain about." She paused and was thinking about another solution.

"I will place an order for a king bed today. That should resolve that problem."

"If you are going to do that, you might want to make sure it has a canopy."

"Pardon?"

"They love the canopy; it makes them feel safe."

"Well George, you did find out a lot about the girls last night. Anything else I should know?"

He lowered his head and held his cup of coffee with two hands before sharing what else he had discovered about his daughter. How she revealed she had experienced some hard times in the System. That information broke his heart and shocked the First Lady. He recognized her maturity and figured it was from being in the System. Being in the pen caused him to man up, so he understood that. Yet, he was amazed at his daughter's intelligence, having overheard her say that she didn't forget much impressed him a lot.

Stating with some surprise. "She shared that she doesn't forget much. That had to be a gift from God, because my folk don't share such a trait and as far as I know her mother's side don't either."

Not sure how to bring up such an unusual fact about his daughter but figured he should share it with the First Lady, seeing how they were alone. Then the bomb shell dropped.

"She said she talks with angels."

The First Lady slowly lowered her coffee cup and stared at George waiting to see what he would say next. George was waiting to see if she would remark on his statement. It was like a mini showdown. When finally, the First Lady made her move.

"George, did you say angels?" She knew very well he said angels, she knows about the angels, but she was hesitant to add to what he may think he heard. And she was curious why Emily shared this knowledge with the girls.

"Yes, in fact they talked all night about angels."

She was in a bit of a shock over this revelation. Where was her husband? He needed to be here to help her with this situation. The girls know. What are they going to ask when they come down this morning? She didn't have the answers that they were likely to ask. Again, where was her husband? Will he get back before they come down? She sat silently, processing many questions in her head, many were the same ones as if on an automatic reel. While George waited patiently for her to respond. When the ice was suddenly broken.

"Ma'am, I didn't mean to shock you. I wasn't sure if you knew about the angel sightings, or not. But Emily seems to know a great deal about them. I don't think she is crazy."

"Crazy?" She looked stunned.

"I mean, Emily isn't insane."

"Of course not." She was shaking her head as if in disgust. Emily had been labeled as a young child and they had to help her through all that when she came to reside with them as their daughter. This was not something she wanted to relive.

"Emily isn't insane, she is gifted." Clarity needed to be set.

CHAPTER THIRTEEN

"Gifted, as in touched?" George was still confused.

"Gifted, as in she has been given a gift from God."

"So, you know about the angels?"

"Yes, we know about the angels, and we know about Emily's calling to deliver messages to people from God. However, we weren't aware that she had shared that information with the twins."

"Not until last night."

"Well, it certainly was a big night for you and the girls." She pondered things for a moment and added. "And a big morning for Jim."

Now worried about how his morning was going. How long was the confrontation going to take? Would he get any answers from Allen? A lot of major shifts were taking place.

"Yeah, I hope he brings that fellow down. We got him on all kinds on charges. But ma'am, you know it goes deeper than one man? I should have taken that one agent out when I had a chance, a car ride wasn't quite enough for attempting to hurt my child. Or you all, of course."

"We got him dead to rights. He isn't going anywhere. However, he may be the one that can point us to the others involved. What do they call that? A snitch?"

George smiled and bobbed his head yes. "That's close enough."

They shared another pot of coffee together when George turned to the First Lady and asked for a favor.

"I know I'm in no position to ask anything of you, but this is more for Emily."

Handing her a letter, then explaining that when something happens to him, he would like for her to give that letter to Emily. Although, it would be better for her to hold onto it, until she is older. It was a list of her living relatives on both sides of the family. He wasn't too proud of where he came from, so he didn't want Emily getting involved with the kinfolk as a child. He explained they would take advantage of her, as he looked around the room noting where they were, wanting her to understand the weight of what he was saying. It was his hope that the President and First Lady would watch over her closely. Preventing any manipulation from his family.

The First Lady was close to tears. It was apparent George was trying to put things in order before he passed, and he was concerned about his daughter. They were right about him; he had a big heart.

"George, You know we will watch over Emily and protect her. And George, you know we are going to take good care of you. We will search everywhere for a donor. We will put you up in the finest hospitals when the time comes."

"I'm not going to any hospital. That would be like putting me back in the pen. It's captivity and I don't want any part of it."

"I never thought of it like that. Oh course, you can stay here, and we will provide care for you right here, with us. That way you will be with Emily."

George was moved by her generosity and kindness, tears welled up, which he wiped away quickly. He didn't want to appear too soft. They heard pitter patter coming their way. George jumped up and started breakfast.

"They'll be hungry."

The First Lady smiled at his willingness to take care of the girls. All three came running to their mom and gave her a big hug. Being home in their own bed had a positive effect on them. All three turned and greeted George with a big, "Good morning."

"We're so happy to be home, and we are so hungry." Came from all three at the same time.

"Coming right up." George smiled.

Emily twirled around and gave George a big hug and then sat down, as if that was her morning routine. George stopped in his tracks, as if he wanted to savor the moment.

The twins asking at the same time, "Where's dad?"

"He isn't back yet. He had a big meeting to tend to this morning."

Seemingly dazed by the late night their response was simple. "Oh, yeah."

The girls sat down at the table and were distracted again, excited to share what had taken place the night before. The First Lady had her eyes on Emily, waiting for her to give her some kind of sign. Emily wasn't connecting with her Mom; she kept her head down low. She knew she had shared an important family secret, without discussing it first with her parents, and she wasn't sure how her mom would react. The twins continued chatting with such excitement, all about angels.

June had brought her picture Bible to the table and said emphatically, "This one is not a complete book, I need one with more words in it."

The First Lady was a little confused but agreed to get her another Bible.

June asked eagerly. "Do you have one? Can I see it now?"

"Of course, I'll go get it." Leaving the room rather puzzled.

She came back in with her Bible and handed it to June. Realizing Emily had something to do with all this. June was flipping the pages expecting the correct chapter to flop open right where she wanted it to be, as if she was flipping to find a picture of a donkey.

"What are you looking for?"

"The story about the donkey seeing the angel."

April piped in with a little giggle. "The donkey talked." Assuming her mother had not heard that story.

"Why yes, it did. And I heard that you all were up all night talking."

Now they all looked surprised. How did mom know that? Did the angels tell her?

"I've decided it's time to get you girls a king-size bed, like the rest of the rooms. What do you think about that?"

They loved the idea of a big bed, and again wondered how mom knew they wanted something like that. They just knew the angels must have told her that they wanted a big bed. But what about the canopy? They didn't want to lose their feeling of security under the canopy. Conversation pursued and mom agreed that it would be no problem to find a king-canopy-bed. There was excitement bubbling at the table, that only ignited their appetites more. The girls turned their attention back to the Bible, wanting to know more about the angels.

June looked at her mom and asked, "Do you know about angels?

April added, "How else did you know about the bed situation?"

The First Lady responded, "Of course I know about angels. They are throughout that Book you are holding."

"How old are they?" April asked. Still having so many questions.

"Hand me that Book sweetie."

As she was opening the Bible, she turned to Job 38:4-7 (NKJV), explaining that angels existed before God created the earth and that they don't die, so they are pretty old. Further noting that they were there cheering on God's creation of the earth from the very beginning.

"Here we go, sometimes it's best just to read His Word out loud. He is talking with a man called Job here." She read it with great emphasis to make a point of the words spoken.

"*'Where were you when I laid the foundations of the earth? Tell Me, if you have understanding. Who determined its measurements? Surely you know! Or who stretched the line upon it? To what were its foundations fastened? Or who laid its cornerstone, When the morning stars sang together, And all the sons of God shouted for joy?'*"

"God has sons?"

"God has one Son, Jesus Christ. The sons here are referring to the angels, God also created the angels as He did all things. He is Elohim the Creator. We are also called His sons and daughters. Let me show you where that is in the Bible, as well."

CHAPTER THIRTEEN

She started flipping through the pages to find a good reference for what she was wanting to share with these eager little minds. While George was placing stacks of pancakes in front of them, which they proceeded to devour. It seemed like they had a bottomless pit that couldn't be filled up. George was hanging on her every word, very interested in what she was sharing.

"Here we go, 2 Corinthians 6:18 (NKJV), *'I will be a Father to you, And you shall be My sons and daughter Says the LORD almighty.'* And let's take a look at 1 John 3:1-3(NKJV). *'Behold what manner of love the Father has bestowed on us, that we should be called children of God! Therefore the world does not know us, because it did not know Him. Beloved, now we are children of God; and it has not yet been revealed what we shall be, but we know that when He is revealed we shall be like Him, for we shall see Him as He is. And everyone who has this hope in Him purifies himself, just as He is pure.'"*

She knew that was a word for George as much as it was for the girls. He needs to hear that he is purified by the blood of Jesus. That Jesus has accepted him as His son. She was on a roll and flipped to more verses. She was amazed that the girls were not only eating up the pancakes, but they were eating up the words being spoken. It warmed her heart.

"I love this one, 1 John 5:1-5 (NKJV), *'Whoever believes that Jesus is the Christ is born of God, and everyone who loves Him who begot also loves him who is begotten of Him. By this we know that we love the children of God, when we love God and keep His commandments. For this is the love of God, that we keep His commandments. And His commandments are not burdensome. For whatever is born of God overcomes the world. And this is the victory that has overcome the world—faith. Who is he who overcomes the world, but he who believes that Jesus is the Son of God?'* And here is one about adoption that I love in Ephesians 1:5-7 (NKJV), *'Having predestined us to adoption as sons by Jesus Christ to Himself, according to the good pleasure of His will, to the praise of the glory of His grace, by which He made us accepted in the Beloved. In Him we have redemption through His blood, the forgiveness of sins, according to the riches of His grace.'"*

"Do you love that one because we are adopted?"

She smiled at June and said, "Yes, I love you very much, as if I had you myself. And I love that God adopted all of us. He laid on my heart that adoption was a way to have a family. If He made room for me in His heart and family, then I could open my heart up to love children needing a home and a family."

It was at this point that Jim had walked in and overheard the conversation going on but didn't want to interrupt them. He finally stepped forward and had his own Scripture verse to share, that defined a bit of his morning. It was also a good one for him to ponder on before making his next move. All eyes popped over to where their dad was standing eager to hear what he had to share.

"Luke 6:35 (AMP), *'Love your enemies and be kind and do good] doing favors so that someone derives benefit from them] and lend, expecting and hoping for nothing in return but considering nothing as lost and despairing of no one; and then your recompense (your reward) will be great (rich, strong, intense, and abundant), and you will be sons of the Most High, for He is kind and charitable and good to the ungrateful and the selfish and wicked.'"*

She locked eyes with him and knew he had been through a lot. Detecting his voice faltering ever so slight. She flipped to where he was reciting and continued when he paused. Wanting to assist her husband the best she could.

"*'So be merciful (sympathetic, tender, responsive, and compassionate) even as your Father is [all these]. Judge not [neither pronouncing judgement nor subjecting to censure], and you will not be judged; do not condemn and pronounce guilty, and you will not be condemned and pronounced guilty; acquit and forgive and release (give up resentment, let it drop), and you will be acquitted and forgiven and released* (Luke 6:36,37 AMP).'"

CHAPTER THIRTEEN

Jim looked on his wife with such appreciation that she was not only beautiful, but she was a godly woman, one that he was very proud of and was happy to have her support.

"While I'm enjoying the dueling verses we have going on here, I have to say judgment is needing to fall on that man. He can't walk free from what he planned against this family, no matter how close you were to him. Got to do time for the crime." George was determined to see all those who intended harm on the family, get what they deserved.

"He won't walk free, he will be held accountable for his crimes, but we can forgive him. Forgiveness is important in our walk with the Lord. He encourages us to forgive others just as He has forgiven us. It is what sets us apart from the rest of the world. It's important to set an example."

Jim looked over at the girls to see if they were taking in what he was saying. Then he quoted Hebrews 8:12 (NIV). "*'For I will forgive their wickedness and will remember their sins no more.'* God forgives because He is a merciful God. He desires for us to follow His ways so that we can be with Him."

His wife joined in, "Jesus bore our sins on the cross, that means he took them from us, they are not counted against us, and we are free from condemnation, punishment, so that we have a place in heaven. If He is willing to do that for us, and set that example, then we should follow and forgive others."

Little June was shaking her head. "I feel terrible, I haven't forgiven some of those people in the orphanage that mistreated us. Do you think I should forgive them?"

That seemed to come out of the blue, but she was sticking with the train of thought.

"That is what we are trying to get across. You are holding that in your heart, only affecting you. It's holding you captive; it is time to let it go. They may not even realize they hurt you. They were just doing the best they could, under the circumstances that they were working under."

Although she was encouraging forgiveness, she picked up on that this was something else she needed to investigate. After hearing about Emily's difficult time in the System and now June spoke of hard times they endured, just what was going on behind closed doors in these government agencies? This may have to be her next project as First Lady not just as their mom.

Jim pointed to, "Matthew 6:14 (NIV), '*For if you forgive other people when they sin against you, your heavenly Father will also forgive you. But if you do not forgive others their sins, your Father will not forgive your sins.*'"

George commented. "That there, sounds kinda harsh. I sure do want to be forgiven, and it seems right selfish of me not to want to forgive someone else. But when they do something as bad as this fellow has done, I just shake my head, I don't know what to think."

Jim stated clearly and sternly. "He and the others will pay for their crimes. God believes in justice and law and order. But we don't have to condemn him, we can show him some grace. '*Be on your guard! If your brother sins, rebuke him; and if he repents forgive him* (Luke 17:3 NASB).'"

There was more that he wanted to share. "Honey, hand me that Bible please."

He flipped to Matthew 5:44-47 (AMP). "'*But I tell you, Love your enemies and pray for those who persecute you, To show that you are the children of your Father Who is in heaven; for He makes His sun rise on the wicked and on the good, and makes the rain fall upon the upright and the wrongdoers [alike]. For if you love those who love you, what reward can you have? Do not even the tax collectors do that?*' It's not always easy, but it's always right. Forgiving someone is a decision you make, choosing to release an offense and not to be controlled by it, brings healing.'"

"I think this is a good time to share that little quote that's stuck in the back of the Bible there, honey. It's by Carol Wimmer, and I think she makes some good points about being a Christian. The girls might like to hear that."

CHAPTER THIRTEEN

He pulled it out and began reading it. He realized he had never heard it before.

"'When I say, 'I am a Christian'
I'm not shouting, 'I've been saved!'
I'm whispering, 'I get lost sometimes
That's why I chose this way'

When I say, 'I am a Christian'
I don't speak with human pride
I'm confessing that I stumble --
needing God to be my guide

When I say, 'I am a Christian'
I'm not trying to be strong.
I'm professing that I'm weak
and pray for strength to carry on

When I say, 'I am a Christian'
I'm not bragging of success
I'm admitting that I've failed
and cannot ever pay the debt

When I say, 'I am a Christian'
I don't think I know it all,
I submit to my confusion
Asking humbly to be taught

When I say, 'I am a Christian'
I'm not claiming to be perfect
My flaws are far too visible
But God believes I'm worth it

When I say 'I am a Christian'
I still feel the sting of pain,
I have my share of heartache
Which is why I seek God's name

When I say, 'I am a Christian'
I do not wish to judge
I have no authority
I only know I'm loved."

"We are a work in progress needing grace. Just trying to be the best that we can be. God says, 'we are worthy'. That He will give us guidance, strength, and comfort when we need it. And it's nice to know that He is always there for us." Another encouragement from mom.

The girls announced they were finished and ready to go out and play. George picked up on the cues, that he needed to follow them, to keep a close eye on them. He looked back at the mess he had created in the kitchen.

The First Lady motioned for him to go on. "The staff will clean up George. Go after the girls. They are your priority."

The First Lady turned to her husband as she poured him a cup of coffee, and asked, "Did we go too deep with the girls, they seemed to get lost there, towards the end?"

"They are children, their attention span is less than an adult. But no, we did not go too deep. We are shaping little minds and helping them develop good character. Character is the most valued asset we have. It's developed throughout our life's journey and shaped by our choices. We haven't had the girls their whole lives, so we need to share with them as the opportunity arises and as often as we can. God will hold us responsible for what He has entrusted to us, yet He will not hold us accountable for opportunities that were never ours."

Jim paused and smiled at his wife. "Let's make the most of the time we have with them. Strengthening their character will shield them to withstand peer pressure and attacks. We want our girls to have a firm foundation in Jesus, so they aren't easily swayed to social norms of society. Which we are apparently battling now."

"I agree our witness is as important, as our teachings. Demonstrations of forgiveness, kindness, faithfulness, and trustworthiness should be how we walk out our days. I'm very proud of you dear, you are setting a good example."

The First Lady was so pleased, that her husband was taking his role as father so seriously. He had always been very methodical in his approach to all things. She loved the way he was taking such good care of them, even when he had some very difficult things to handle on his own. She held her cup in both hands, took a sip of coffee, pondering whether she should ask how things went or just let him bring it up.

"Yes, I remember you once said that Jesus was 'the Gold Standard.' And that we need to reflect that same spiritual shine and value of gold from our hearts. Then let our actions reflect our hearts. Even if it means, being put to the test of fire, to burn away the impurities, just as gold is refined. I'm feeling the burn. I've been tested this week." Jim was a strong man, but the events of the day were wearing on him.

"I know it's been hard on all of us, but let's focus on Jesus' message, which was to teach us how to have a joy filled and enriched life. Which may mean displaying humility, hunger after right living, being merciful, and even being peacemakers during persecution. Let's show how we believe in Jesus' way. The world is watching us." She was trying to be encouraging.

"I was once told a quote by a gifted man, Martin Luther King Jr., that went something like this, 'The ultimate measure of a man is not where he stands in moments of comfort and convenience, but where he stands at times of challenge and controversy.' I plan to stand tall in these times, I'll let the light of Jesus shine, while I will seek Jesus for guidance. Heaven knows this country needs healing."

She opened the Bible once more for a Word to share from 2 Chronicles 7:14 (NKJV).

"*If My people who are called by My name will humble themselves, and pray and seek My face, and turn from their wicked ways, then I will hear from heaven, and will forgive their sin and heal their land.*"

This day was starting out with great promise.

"When You Speak" by Jeremy Camp

Chapter Fourteen

Justice

The afternoon rolled around, and every radio and television channel were buzzing about the arrest of the Vice President. They of course were getting most of their information from the one media outlet that the President had promised an exclusive interview with. He wanted the truth delivered, not someone's spin on it. The media had gotten to the point of twisting facts and making them fit their narrative. President Patterson was hoping that if he spoke to his source, they would put the truth out first and the rest would have to play catch up. That part of the plan was working smoothly.

The President wanted to assure the people that all those involved in this attempt to remove a sitting president, the one they elected, would be held accountable. He mentioned Proverbs 29:16 (AMP) *"When the wicked are in authority, transgression increases, but the [uncompromising] righteous shall see the fall of the wicked."* This is what he was assuring them. Justice would be sought, and the fullest extent of the law would be handed down. But he would show mercy and forgive on a personal level, because that is the way Christ would have wanted us to move forward. He explained that at times people give in to pressures that surround them, that power can go to one's head, which corrupts their thoughts and actions. He was assuring them that he was staying grounded and that he was moving forward with his agenda, to bring people back around to a righteous walk with God and for the country to thrive under His hand, with the support of his administration.

He declared the importance of electing godly men and women. Once they got to Washington, they need to be prayed for, that they are not tempted and diverted from their assignments for the people. Washington is not a place for personal gain, it is a place to serve the nation and work for its constituent, citizens of the nation. Politicians should remain in the service of the people, giving the people a voice.

"We battle on our knees in prayer and rise to take action in a just manner. We rule and reign with the Lord, in this life and in the next. Let's put our best foot forward in this life and move this country into a more prosperous thriving future. We are told in Luke 19:13 (NKJV), *'Occupy till I come.'* Yes, we are to continue His works with the gifts that He has given us, until our Lord comes back. But the strong word used there is, 'occupy', it's used in the military, it's a word used with force behind it. We should be a strong people, a force to be reckoned with."

He continued after the cheers settled down. "We determine our future; we determine who serves us in an elected position, and we will remove those that are not suited for the job. It's time for warrior hearts to rise, put on the full armor of God and prepare for battle against evil attempts and plots against us."

Jim believes strongly that nothing is too big for God. And he was feeling empowered by God as he spoke to the people he governs over. He had thought out just what to say to encourage them.

"God has said He is with us, He provides help, He loves us, we have life in Him. Listen carefully to John 14:13-21 (NIV), *'Whatever you ask in My name, that will I do, so that the Father may be glorified in the Son. If you ask Me anything in My name, I will do it. If you love Me, you will keep My commandments. I will ask the Father, and He will give you another Helper, that He may be with you forever; that is the Spirit of truth, whom the world cannot receive, because it does not see Him or know Him, but you know Him because He abides with you and will be in you. I will not leave you as orphans; I will come to you. After a little while the world will no longer see Me, but you will see Me; because I live, you will live also. In that day you will know that I am in My Father, and you in Me, and I in you. He who has My commandments and keeps them is the one who loves Me; and he who loves Me will be loved by My Father, and I will love him and will disclose Myself to Him."*

He looked on at the reporters that were seeking his attention, and he knew that he wasn't going to miss this opportunity to get his statement out over a huge audience. He smiled and continued boldly.

"I have proven myself to you. I speak boldly the name of the Lord to you. I have run this race with the Lord's influence. It has put the country on the right track. We as a people have made a difference in our schools, giving the power back to the parents where it belongs. We have cleansed the curriculum, removing the absurd agenda brainwashing our children and polluting their minds, by welcoming our faith back in the doors to shape our children according to God's plans for them. And yes, we are respecting our flag and those that serve this country in the military. It's your actions that are making a difference and creating a future for our children."

It was important to remind the people how far they have come.

"Business is flourishing nationwide because of the regulations being removed, taxes being lowered, and the workforce expansion is underway. Legislation has improved the infrastructure; our streets are safer than ever before. This nation will not crumble because of the actions of a few."

The crowd was wanting more information, so he continued with hope for the people.

"I will seek a good and desirable person to work alongside me, to finish my assignment as President of this great nation. My requirement will be that they be spiritual minded and follow Gods will. We are fighting an ideological war that requires spiritual warfare. We should all seek to be surrounded by like-minded people for spiritual development. You've heard the expression 'iron sharpens iron'. Use the influence you have in your own sphere, look inward and seek what God has called you to do where you live. You can make a difference; you have proven that already. Let's continue to build on that together. We are building something that will stand the test of time to come, a future."

The girls were excited to see their Dad on the television. It was a reminder how important a position he held which kept him very busy. It's why they treasured the time that he carved out, just for them. They were thankful for having such a respected man as their father. They referred to him often as 'The President or Mr. President' because they were so proud of him. Emily had known the honor that her father felt, to be called the President, because he was first Dad, to her. The twins knew him first as the President, before calling him Dad.

It was time for class. The First Lady, their mom and teacher, shut the television off and asked the question about classwork. They were being homeschooled. The schools had improved greatly, but it was still best for their safety if they remained with her and a security detail. At times, they would have special tutors come in, to assist the First Lady when she had obligations to meet. It was her distinct pleasure to teach her girls, even if they were not at the White House, this had been her plan for Emily. Lesson plans were made easier that the girls were all pretty much on the same level of studies. Emily was just challenged a bit more with her work.

CHAPTER FOURTEEN

Emily inquired when her mom turned the television off. "Aren't we watching history being made?" She was eager to watch more of her dad on television.

She smiled and answered in the affirmative but insisted on the history books.

"We live in a place of power and influence, but there is no authority above God. Our Founding Fathers knew that. When they built many of the buildings surrounding us, they recognized that and placed evidence of it. I'll have to point some of those things out on our next field trip."

That got the girls attention. They loved field trips, but she knew there was always a lot of work and planning involved in their outings. She continued to share about their heritage as Believers.

"Moses and the Ten Commandments are displayed on the building where the Supreme Court presides. As you enter the Supreme Court courtroom the two huge doors have the Ten Commandments engraved on each lower portion of the doors. It's also displayed above where the judges sit. I imagine they thought the Ten Commandments were important to follow if they gave them such a place of distinction. And there are Bible verses etched in stone all over the Federal Buildings and Monuments throughout Washington. It will be fun looking for them and seeing which ones are used."

"Kinda like an Easter egg hunt." April giggled.

"We will make it fun as we learn." She replied.

"Would it surprise you to know that fifty-two of the fifty-five founders of the Constitution were members of the established orthodox churches in the colonies. And that they prayed before every session of Congress. This is what your father is talking about, trying to reestablish faith in our leadership. Even Patrick Henry, a Founding Father of our country stated, 'It cannot be emphasized too strongly or too often that this great nation was founded not by religionists but by Christians, not by religions but on the Gospel of Jesus Christ.'"

"I brought my Bible to class; I want to read stories in it during our quiet time today." Stated June with enthusiasm.

The First Lady looked up and noticed her husband standing there waiting patiently. So, it was thought that this was a good time for that quiet time reading. Instructing them to pull out their reading materials and she would be back in a little while. Promising that they were going to start something new and exciting.

The First Lady walked into his home office, and he quietly shut the door behind them.

"You are doing such a great job with them." He stated proudly.

"Well, I never thought I'd be a teacher, but I really am enjoying the interaction with the girls about different topics. I love the preparation work it takes. It's like going to school all over again. There is a wonderful support team for the homeschoolers, which has been very helpful and takes some of the fear out of teaching."

"I'm glad to hear that. It's important that parents have a say and take part in their children's education. I'm sure it helps to have others to talk to for some guidelines."

She could tell that he was drifting, something else was on his mind. "You have something to share, dear."

"I just keep thinking about Allen and how to handle what needs to happen next. I know that God uses all kinds of people for His purposes. Isaiah 45 tells us that. It may be that He used Allen to encourage me to run for office, his help did catapult me in place. And look at all we were able to get done in such a short time. But how did things go so wrong? This is what stumps me."

"God did orchestrate all this. I just don't know what happened to Allen. Your assignment can still be accomplished."

"Yes, we can still move on with our assignment without him. We are here to reclaim this country for the people and advance God's Word. These past few years, we've been able to shine a light on a lot of corruption and have been able to conduct a major cleanup. Getting us on the right path with the Founding Fathers. I heard you talking about that with the girls."

"Yeah, they are excited about a fieldtrip now."

"I might want to join you on that Easter egg hunt." They both laughed.

"It's important that the girls understand what we are doing here. How we've stood with the Founding Fathers and the Constitution, how we are following Law and Order, and we're promoting a good life for all Americans. This nation was founded on the love of God, and He desires to continue to bless us for that. I was reading Isaiah 43:19 (NLT), earlier and thought it hit home with me. *'I am about to do something new. See, I have already begun! Do you not see it? I will make a pathway through the wilderness. I will create rivers in the dry wasteland.'* I will not stand for people riding the fence, they are either for us, or against us. I plan to dethrone evil, and its agenda against humanity. I will work something new for this country that stands for God's purposes. God has proven that we are not invisible to Him, so we need to show that He is not invisible to us. This will be important in my selection of a new Vice President."

The First Lady opened her Bible that she had been carrying around from the classroom and turned to Psalm 33:12 (NKJV), "*'Blessed is the nation whose God is the LORD, the people He has chosen as His own inheritance.'* This nation shall be blessed, there was a covenant with the Founding Fathers that will not be forgotten. We are carrying the banner today, and we need to trust in the Lord, that all things will work out."

Looking back down at the Bible, she flipped to Proverbs 3:5-8 (NKJV), "*'Trust in the Lord with all your heart, and lean not on your own understanding, In all your ways acknowledge Him, and He shall direct your paths. Do not be wise in your own eyes; fear the LORD and depart from evil. It will be health to your flesh, and strength to your bones.'*"

"You are right, dear. We will be established in His Will and take His agenda to the streets. We don't have to understand how it's going to happen; we just need to trust and obey. Culture infiltrated our churches and corrupted them with their lies. I know that is how this all got started. We are going to infiltrate every aspect of culture and make a difference for God's purposes, from the highest office in the land." He slammed his fist on the desk startling his wife.

Unaware of his own enthusiasm he went on to quote Joshua 24:15 (NIV). "*'But if serving the LORD seems undesirable to you, then choose for yourselves this day who you will serve, whether the gods your ancestors served beyond the Euphrates, or the gods of the Amorites, in whose land you are living. But as for me and my household, we will serve the LORD.'*"

"Yes dear, We will serve the LORD." She smiled back at him.

He became pensive once again. "But what am I to do with Allen?"

It was always his way to rely on the wise counsel of his wife, it was why he had come back to his home office instead of heading to the oval office. He trusted her counsel more right now than any other.

Opening the Bible to Romans 12:17-21 (NIV) she began to read. "*'Do not repay anyone evil for evil. Be careful to do what is right in the eyes of everyone. If it is possible, as far as it depends on you, live at peace with everyone. Do not take revenge, my dear friends, but leave room for God's wrath, for it is written: 'It is mine to avenge; I will repay' says the Lord. On the contrary: If your enemy is hungry, feed him; if he is thirsty, give him something to drink. In doing this, you will heap burning coals on his head. Do not be overcome by evil, but overcome evil with good.'*"

"How do you know right where to turn in the Bible?"

"Because I stay in the Word, and because I've had to look it up several times. I struggle with all this as well, just like everyone else. I know what's right, but at times, I have to be reminded, and I take comfort in reading it from His Word. Just like I'm strengthened by Paul's words, telling us how God uses us. Listen to 2 Corinthians 2:14,15 (NCV), '*God uses us to spread his knowledge *everywhere like a sweet-smelling perfume. Our offering to God is this: We are the sweet smell of Christ among those who are being saved and among those who are being lost.'* Christ wants us to live our lives so that no matter, our location, and station in life, we are disseminating the sweet-smelling perfume of the gospel, which then rises up to glorify God. It's important that we exhibit His character in everything we do and say, that our life draws others to Him. This is our assignment from God."

"So, we are to be about our assignment, and let God handle the wrath part?"

"Yes, ultimate justice belongs at His throne. Our courts will handle what happens to Allen and the others here. You don't have to wear all the hats. You are the President, in a position to lead, not dispense justice, nor to micromanage others."

"As President, and one that is to set an example for others, I think we need to work on our own household."

"What do you mean dear?" Unsure of the direction he was wanting to go into, their family were Believers and they had George converted.

"I had not noticed how far Allen slipped from his faith into a cesspool of corruption. He was my inner circle, which is like my household. I think that we need to focus on getting our house in order, Gods order, as a demonstration and then our outreach will manifest exponentially."

"You mean like Peter preaching the message to Cornelius's family and the whole household was saved."

"Yes, but I'm aware that they still must believe for themselves. Our attitude and actions are what matters to God, not our station in life. I desire all under my care to know Jesus. It's about promoting peace and reconciliation among us. I fear that Allen's actions may sway people's beliefs and we must shore up our household's faith first, so that we are not divided here in any way."

"That makes me think of Jesus' Word in Matthew 10, let me flip there. *'Whoever acknowledges me before others, I will also acknowledge before my Father in heaven. But whoever disowns me before others, I will disown before my Father in heaven. Do not suppose that I have come to bring peace to the earth. I did not come to bring peace, but a sword. For I have come to turn 'a man against his father, a daughter against her mother, a daughter-in-law her mother-in -law—a man's enemies will be the members of his own household.' Anyone who loves their father or mother more than me is not worthy of me; anyone who loves their son or daughter more than me is not worthy of me. Whoever does not take up their cross and follow me is not worthy of me. Whoever finds their life will lose it, and whoever loses their life for my sake will find it* (Matthew 10:32-39 NIV).'"

She closed the Book. "Honey you are simply acknowledging Jesus and making Him known as your King and establishing that you will govern by His ways. I think a household of faith is the proper approach, although, you are correct in saying that each one has to come to know and accept Christ on their own. We can simply give them the opportunity to feast on the Word and then they need to respond. Hopefully by taking it back to their families like with the Philippian jailer that Paul shared the Gospel with, in Acts 16:34 (NASB). *'He brought them into his house and set food before them, and rejoiced greatly, having believed in God with his whole household.'"*

"I guess I want them all to understand, that we all mess up, but if you know God the Father as a loving Dad, then they can always run to Him for help and forgiveness. Don't run away from Him. Just as they can come to me, and we can work through what their problems are or clean up their messes together. I'm here to lead but I can also be the one to help them with solutions to their problems."

"You're a good man, Mr. President."

He came around his desk and gave her a big hug, thanking her for her help.

She then stated as she was excusing herself. "I have something new to get started with the girls."

"What might that be, my dear?"

"Prayer walks. We are confined a bit here, until the media settles down and quits trying to get to the girls for comments. Good grief, they are children and should be off limits."

"So, what do you mean by prayer walks?" He asked, now more interested.

"We are going to walk the halls and pray for all the people who stayed here. We will talk about the different presidents and their families, while we thank them for their service to the nation and things that they accomplished while in office."

"Sounds like you might have some homework to do before tackling that job."

"Yeah, but I love history and it won't be a chore. I've already studied up on some."

"That's going to be a great witness to the staff which is part of what I was talking about."

"Yeah, I kind of feel that way as well."

"What are you going to do when you finish with the house?"

"We will take it to the streets. Lift prayers for those businesses around us, the people that work there, parks, churches, basically praying for the community, then the city, then the nation. There are always things to pray for. We did this in our neighborhood when I was growing up. You'd be surprised how effective it was for our community."

"Sounds like you put some thought into this."

"I actually gave it some thought before we were in lockdown here. I just hadn't gotten around to implementing it. My goal is to get the girls use to praying for others, and if I can get them to seek passages that apply to where we are going, then I've got their noses in the Bible and the history books. There is always hope that they will memorize the Scriptures, that way it's always with them."

"And of course, learning history while they are at it, I get what you are doing."

She smiled. She knew he got it, they could learn more by doing this than from merely memorizing history points.

"It's to bring awareness of our community, where we live. In a big city there are many needs. We can lift-up prayer for peace, for well-being and health, protection, and safety, but also their salvation. Look how we impacted George's life. It makes me want to witness and bring everyone to Jesus. That's why I love your plan so much, dear."

"While you are at it, can you rebuke the sin and work of Satan in this town?"

"Yes, that they turn from darkness to light. I've got some verses to start them out on, then I'll let them dig in the Scriptures for more. It will be fun to see what they find."

She outlined a few of the Scriptures she had pulled together. Hoping to get his input on them.

"What do you think about James 5:15,16 (NKJV), '*The prayer of faith will save the sick, and the Lord will raise him up. And if he has committed sins, he will be forgiven. Confess your trespasses to one another and pray for one another, that you may be healed. The effective, fervent prayer of a righteous man avails much.*'

And an easy one to remember would be Mark 12:31 (NKJV), '*You shall love your neighbor as yourself.*'

I find Isaiah 32:18 (NKJV) comforting, '*My people will dwell in a peaceful habitation, In secure dwellings, and in quiet resting places.*' What do you think?"

"This is going to stir up the spiritual realm in DC." The President responded with enthusiasm. "Emily's angel is going to love your new plan."

She loved the fact that they thought so much alike. This was a spiritual battle plan, that the whole family could be involved in. They had watched the

CHAPTER FOURTEEN

deterioration of the nation over several decades to the point it was as if it were on life support. Freedoms were slipping away and getting lost in unconstitutional mandates. They knew that they were to be a part of the revival of this nation. They couldn't avoid the crisis the nation had been in. It needed recitation, new breath of life to cross the country. They were going to be that breath of fresh air and hope. They were going to speak truth.

The President and First Lady had been key figures in pointing out problem areas and finding solutions. Most concerns were resolved with faith and biblical principles. Statements from the Founding Fathers were used in many cases, to demonstrate the roots that the country started from.

They particularly loved to quote Thomas Jefferson, and it was funny how he seemed to know that the country would decline and need to hear his words again: "Injustice in government undermines the foundations of a society. A nation, therefore, must take measures to encourage its members along the paths of justice and morality. I think myself that we have more machinery of government than is necessary, too many parasites living on the labor of the industrious. Government big enough to supply everything you need is big enough to take everything you have…The course of history shows that as a government grows, liberty decreases. The two enemies of the people are criminals and government, so let us tie the second down with the chains of the constitution so the second will become the legalized version of the first."

Dependent people are easily controlled, and DC wanted more power, so it had begun crippling the people. This was to change.

"Our liberty depends on the freedom of the press, and that cannot be limited without being lost." These were wise words spoken by Thomas Jefferson to Dr. James Currie, in 1786.

The President and First Lady had spoken boldly of the press, and how it had been bought off, bribed, or threatened, therefore staining the country with lies and propaganda. The press had become a tool of deception and needed to be listened to with a great deal of discernment. They had shed light on this matter as they crossed the nation. Where there is light and truth, there is cleansing.

He also pointed out that a change of heart was needed, it became part of his campaign. The country had become divisive, and they needed to unite as one again, be proud to be an American. What had become of patriotism? Thomas Jefferson had stated, "A true patriot will defend his country from its government." This was their agenda.

He explained to the public the importance of one's journey through life, how one treats and respects their neighbor, can affect a community. It was encouraged to override your emotions and make a decision with your soul, on how to react towards others. He had stated many a time, to embrace the motto, "One nation under God."

And he used Thomas Jeffersons words, "The reason that Christianity is the best friend of government is because Christianity is the only religion that changes the heart."

Scripture that was cited from his stump, all across the nation moved people in the right direction. *"If my people who are called by My name humble themselves, and pray and seek My face, and turn from their wicked ways, then I will hear from heaven, and will forgive their sin and heal their land* (2 Chronicles 7:14 NKJV)."

Song "Gifts from God" by Chris Tomlin ft. Chris Lane

Chapter Fifteen

Heaven's Conclusion

Months passed; the trials revealed all those that were involved in the plans to remove the President from office. A house cleaning had to be conducted in the Secret Service. Too many agents were easily paid off to commit the unthinkable crimes.

At the cabin, there had only been one rouge agent, that was waiting on the right time to take the shot to kill the President. He had to be careful not to arouse suspension from the other agents. When the family bolted from the house, he had been strategically located to target the President before he got to the car for any reason. It would have been excused as an attempt to shoot an intruder, that would coincidently never be found. His testimony was startling, the rouge agent had the President in his sights, he fired, but something prevented him from being hit. It couldn't be explained. Once his shot was fired, the other agents fired as in a chain reaction at the car, trying to stop it. They were unaware of what was actually going down at the time.

The agent at the safe house had been reamed out by the Vice President, for not getting enough poison in the food that was delivered to the family. He had been called in to try again, and threatened that he'd better get it right, even if he opened fire on the family. It had been stated that they would cover it up somehow, afterwards. Or could it be that he was to be used as a scape goat.

It was apparent that the Vice President was antsy and had gotten a bit sloppy. He was being pushed for time. Having no idea how long the President would follow his advice and stay in seclusion. At some point Jim would want to come back to town, where it would be harder to cover up any incident.

The agent that had been hit from behind with a car and left injured in the ditch was discovered by the other agents after they had changed the slashed tires and headed out after the family. George had hoped that he had taken care of at least one fool for good. A decision had to made spontaneously by the agents, help him get to a hospital, or take out after the family. At which point, they really had no idea which direction to go. These agents were involved with the murder scheme of the family. They had been bought and paid for and told there would be cover for them. They had been given their orders from the top, to keep an eye on the family, until the right time. When George had shown up and gone inside, they had assumed he was the one selected to carry out the plan, and they would be there for the coverup and the cover story.

All trials were aired by every kind of media and headline news. The girls were kept from the television and monitored carefully during these events. They didn't want anyone asking them questions and dragging them into the drama.

They had enough to deal with in their own household. George's health was failing. As promised, he was being cared for in their home with excellent healthcare workers and doctors that made house calls. The girls visited with him daily. They did their best to keep his spirits up. The First Lady spent a lot

CHAPTER FIFTEEN

of time with him, encouraging him and letting him know as a Believer in Jesus Christ, he had nothing to fear, he was just preparing for a wonderful transition.

One night she opened the balcony doors to let in some fresh air, enabling George to see the night sky so that he wouldn't feel so confined. As she gazed up at the twinkling lights, she proceeded to tell him about how God named all the stars in the sky, each with its own story. Explaining that God placed His Gospel for His people in the night sky, for them to share with each generation. She pulled up Scripture to back up what she was telling him.

"Psalm 19:1 (AMP), '*The heavens declare the glory of God; and the firmament shows and proclaims His handiwork.*' It's telling us that he provided us a way to remember what He has done. He is the great Creator after all."

Flipping to the beginning of the Bible. "Genesis 1:14,16 (NKJV), '*And God said, 'Let there be lights in the firmament of the heavens to divide the day from the night; and let them be for signs and for seasons, and for days and years;' Then God made two great lights; the greater light to rule the day, and lesser light to rule the night. He made the stars also.*'"

She continued with further explanation. "According to tradition, the signs came from Seth, the son of Adam, and Enoch, the son of Cain. So, the message was revealed by God to Adam, then passed down through civilizations throughout the world for centuries. They've all shared the same story."

George chimed in, "I know about those constellations. Don't people read horoscopes and think they can predict something about themselves?"

"They do, but man corrupted the Zodiac into a satanic counterfeit. It's so typical for man to distort something that God meant for good. Man changed it into deities and began to worship the sun, moon, and stars. Satan is always trying to get man to look elsewhere, to take your mind and worship off God. But Zodiac actually means path, which is the Way of Salvation. And we know that Jesus is the only Way. God wanted us to have a way to always see Christ before us."

"You mean it's kinda like a picture book, laid out in the stars, right there above us, telling us Jesus' story?"

"Yes, it's quite beautiful. I'll find the book that I like to reference, it's called, "The Real Meaning Of The Zodiac," by Dr. James Kennedy, Ph.D., and we'll go through each constellation and see if we can spot it in the night sky. It starts with His birth and goes all the way through His crucifixion, a message of redemption, even the part of Christ coming for His church and His Judgment. The first one we will look for is Cancer, the Crab. I think we will be able to spot it soon."

"Why a crab?"

"A crab lives in two elements, water and land. The church lives in two elements as well, the earth and also in heaven. I think of it as stated in John 17:14 (NASB), '*I have given them Your word; and the world has hated them, because they are not of the world, even as I am not of the world.*' I love the fact that Jesus wants to protect us from that hate and includes us in His glory. Listen to the way He put it. '*The glory which You have given Me I have given to them, that they may be one, just as We are one; in them and You in Me, that they may be perfected in unity, so that the world may know that You sent Me, and loved them, even as You have loved Me* (John 17:22,23 NASB).' That love is meant to be a comfort to us all."

"I know it's a comfort to me, you all have been such a comfort as well." George was looking weak.

The First Lady continued, not sure how to respond right then without tears bubbling up.

"The word cancer actually means, 'The Traveler's Resting Place for the Encircled', or 'embraced'. It represents the completion of the Redeemer's work. Christ possesses or embraces the church and has reserved a place in heaven for us all, our resting place. There is a nebulous cluster, in the midst of Cancer, called Praesepe, which means 'the multitude or the offspring'. That's us, we are

CHAPTER FIFTEEN

represented in the sky as one of the brightest in all the heavens, for all the world to see. We are meant to let our light shine bright."

"Are we looking for the crab, because you know that I am going on to Heaven soon?"

"It's true that you may be embracing your resting place soon, but I was thinking that it would be easy to spot this time of year. We can't see the entire story at one time in the night sky, we have to seek what is visible to us." Thinking there was a lesson in there as well.

"Oh, well that's good, too."

It was getting late; his eyes lids were starting to droop signaling he was getting tired. She was glad to have found something that they could discuss each night. She was going to look for that book and some binoculars to prepare for tomorrow night. The girls were doing their part by sharing what they had been up to each day, covering each detail with great enthusiasm. Then they'd take turns reading Bible stories to him, to wind down his night, and theirs.

The next morning the President decided to have coffee with George, in his room. It was mostly discussion about sports, until the topic got deeper with questions of, 'What if's' occurred. What if, our paths were different? What if, George had been dealt a different hand? What if, he was still married and was able to raise Emily with his wife? Who had died just a few years after his incarceration. He shook his head, knowing that things wouldn't have turned out all that much better, unless he had found Jesus earlier. The projection of his life had been different, but Jesus had pursued him, and he was grateful.

Jim asked the question, "If you had endless time and money, what would you have wanted to do with it?"

"Easy, I always wanted to have my own ranch. A big spread with cattle and horses."

"Were you ever a cowhand?" Surprised by his choice of dream jobs.

"For a while, I worked someone else's spread, I liked the freedom of being on the land."

"What happened?"

"Trouble followed me, everywhere I went."

"A cowboy, eh? Didn't see that one coming." They laughed. "Laughter is good medicine for the soul as stated in Proverbs 17:22. Just as *'Gracious words are a honeycomb, sweet to the soul and healing to the bones.'* from Proverbs 16:24 (NIV)."

Emily was outside the room and overheard her dads' dreams. She knew she wanted to get him a cowboy hat as soon as she could. She wanted to make his dreams come true and thought the hat would make him feel like a cowboy. She hurried off to see how she could make it happen.

Deciding to involve the twins in her plans made it a bigger project. April painted him a masterpiece on a sheet from their bed. They were going to hang it up on his wall where he could look at his ranch from his bed. Emily, with the help of her mother, purchased his hat and had it special delivered.

Preparations were made for a big celebration, to present their gifts to George. June was going to play a 'June original' on the violin, for him. The First Lady ordered up a 'ranchers special' for dinner. The biggest steak they could find, cooked just the way he liked it, no green stuff on his plate. It brought back memories of when George provided them with a much-appreciated meal, on the run. This was such a good plan and God was allowing everything to fall into place perfectly. If George could just hold out a little while longer.

The celebration day finally came, the masterpiece was finished, the gift was wrapped, and the song was composed. The whole family was excited about the surprise they were bringing George. The staff were included in the plans and shared in the excitement and joy, thrilled with the family's preparations for George.

CHAPTER FIFTEEN

There was big pomp and ceremony with horns blowing, as they marched into his room to hang the masterpiece on the wall. The violin played, while they presented him with his gift of a cowboy hat, and then the dinner followed on a big silver platter. They had spared no expense. It was a fine celebration and a moment of great joy and lots of smiles. George was overwhelmed with all the love that was demonstrated.

"George, don't you know that all of heaven will show up for you when you make it home. The celebration will be so much more than what we have done here."

"I'm grateful for everything, I really am. This has been the best day ever." He was fighting back tears but grinning as big as a Cheshire cat.

When things settled down, the girls went off to bed. Everyone was pleased how things went. Emily had a huge smile on her face, she just knew everything was going to be alright. The First Lady had stayed with George, to just sit with him quietly after all the excitement. She had a feeling that things might be closer than the girls realized.

George leaned towards her and asked the question, "What do you think it will be like?"

"Heaven?" She asked.

"Yes."

"I know there is nothing to fear. You won't go alone. Angels will carry you to Heaven. Jesus himself may be the one to welcome you. Listen to John 14:2,3 (NASB), *'In My Father's house are many dwelling places; if it were not so, I would have told you; for I go to prepare a place for you. If I go and prepare a place for you, I will come again and receive you to Myself, that where I am, there you may be also.'* God has prepared a place just for you, George. Isaiah 32:18 (NIV) says, *'My people will live in peaceful dwelling places, in secure homes, in undisturbed places of rest.'* And Proverbs 24:3 (NIV) adds, *'By wisdom a house is built, and through understanding it is established; through knowledge its rooms are filled with rare and beautiful treasures.'"*

"I think all my treasure is right here." As he looked around the room at his gifts and embraced the love that had been poured out on him.

She allowed him time to picture just what she had read to him. Then she shared with him a quote. "Billy Graham once said, 'My home is in Heaven. I'm just traveling through this world.' You have finished your travels, George. You are headed home. Where love will fill every room. You are passing into a new beginning of life. A life that has no end. You will be welcomed with open arms by all those who went before you. The heavenly host will sing and celebrate."

"Like what we did tonight?"

"I believe it will be much bigger. What we see here and experience here is only a faint image of what Heaven is all about. Here it's like seeing a reflection or an impression of what's above, yet in Heaven all is magnified with brilliance and clarity. Heaven is bigger than our imaginations. After all, God isn't limited, He created all things here and above. Can't you imagine that He saved the best for His own dwelling place? So, whatever you can dream up, He has already thought it, and created it. Earth just wasn't big enough for all that He has created. I'm sure there is limitless activity and places to explore, like your ranch. Imagine looking through time; past, present, and future and having the ability to experience it all. We've only lived a glimpse of time; heaven is eternal time."

Pausing a minute wanting him to grasp everything being said. She saw his smile and knew she could continue. He was visualizing what she was describing. They were in no hurry.

"That's just what your eyes will take in. Your heart will be full, filled with love and acceptance, that can't be experience here. No matter how much we try to show love here, it will be magnified so much more in Heaven. You will be wrapped and able to bask in the love of the Father, His Son, and all those who surround them. You are literally filled with joy and full of happiness, and you will experience great peace. Jesus's captivating light will shine everywhere; you will truly be enveloped in His light and His Glory."

George was intently listening as she painted a picture with her words. You could almost see the excitement in his eyes. The fear had left him.

"George, I want you to know I'm not making this up, everything I'm talking about is Scriptural. In 1 Corinthians 13:12 (TLB) it states, '*In the same way, we can see and understand only a little about God now, as if we were peering at his reflection in a poor mirror; but someday we are going to see Him in His completeness, face to face. Now all that I know is hazy and blurred, but then I will see everything clearly, just as clearly as God sees into my heart right now.*'

And Revelation 22:5 (NIV) states, '*There will be no more night. They will not need the light of a lamp or the light of the sun, for the Lord God will give them light. And they will reign forever and ever.*'"

"You've done a good job comforting me. The kids put on quite the party for me. I'm very happy and at peace."

He looked over at the masterpiece hanging on his wall, and over at the big cowboy hat on the bedside table. Still hearing the tune in his head that June composed. He looked over at the First Lady staring out the balcony window and commented on what a wonderful family she has. And that she was surely blessed.

That was sweet words coming from a man who had recently found Jesus. "I think the girls reading has gotten to you, George."

They both smiled. Then George asked the question, "How about another one of those star pictures. Have you found one, out the window there?" His voice was giving way to a whisper.

"What about Argo, the Ship." She hadn't actually found it, but she thought it would be a good one to share at this time.

"It represents a ship that has finished its journey, it's at rest. Christ is the captain of that ship. He is bringing it home, safely to rest in its harbor. There is also, a lion on that ship, that represents the Lion of Judah, he is protecting and watching over His own, seeing that one finds his rest by the Redeemer."

"I think, I will enjoy that ship." He said softly as if his voice was sailing off.

She proceeded to read Psalm 34:20-22 (NKJV). "*Our soul waits for the LORD; He is our help and our shield. For our heart shall rejoice in Him, Because we have trusted in His holy name. Let Your mercy, O LORD, be upon us, Just as we hope in You.*"

She flipped over to Psalm 100:1-5 (NKJV) to continue to read. Knowing that he enjoyed listening to her melodious voice. It soothed him to sleep many nights.

"*Make a joyful shout to the LORD, all you lands! Serve the LORD with gladness; Come before His presence with singing. Know that the LORD, He is God; It is He who has made us, and not we ourselves; We are His people and the sheep of His pasture. Enter into His gates with thanksgiving, And into His courts with praise. Be thankful to Him, and bless His name. For the LORD is good; His mercy is everlasting, And His truth endures to all generations.*"

George passed peacefully, surrounded by his treasures of the day.

Song "My Jesus" Anne Wilson

Chapter Sixteen

Good News

The First Lady had stayed the night with George knowing that his time was coming to an end, and she didn't want him to be alone. It was a difficult morning, breaking the news to everyone, including the staff. Everyone had gone to bed on such a joyous note, to have then woke to such sorrow.

"Why did God not answer my prayer to heal George?" Emily asked through tears.

"God hears our prayers, and He answers them according to His will. It might not be the answer we are looking for. But His timing is perfect. Emily, God did heal George, his sins were washed clean, and he was given access to Jesus in heaven, where there is no illness or pain, he is healed completely. There is eternal life, life with no end. God speaks in His Word about a time to live and a time to die. George ran his race on this earth, and it was time to go home, where God prepared a place for him. We should take comfort in knowing that God has our lives ordered on His timeline. He never lets us out of His sight. He was there at the moment we were conceived, and He will be there to welcome us home when it's our time. Let me read you a Scripture that I find comfort in."

She opened her Bible and turned to Psalm 139:1-6,13-18 (NASB), and began to read.

"'*O LORD, You have searched me and known me. You know when I sit down and when I rise up; You understand my thought from afar. You scrutinize my path and my lying down, And are intimately acquainted with all my ways. Even before there is a word on my tongue, Behold, O LORD, You know it all. You have enclosed me behind and before, And laid Your hand upon me. Such knowledge is too wonderful for me; It is too high, I cannot attain to it.*

For You formed my inward parts; You wove me in my mother's womb. I will give thanks to You, for I am fearfully and wonderfully made; Wonderful are Your works, And my soul knows it very well. My frame was not hidden from You, When I was made in secret, And skillfully wrought in the depths of the earth; Your eyes have seen my unformed substance; And in Your book were all written The days that were ordained for me, When as yet there was not one of them. How precious also are Your thoughts to me, O God! How vast is the sum of them! If I should count them, they would outnumber the sand. When I awake, I am still with You.'"

"Why does He have to take us home?"

"I imagine He has prepared great things for us in heaven, that He wants us to enjoy. Now can you imagine the earth being filled with humanity that never dies, yet we still have children, after thousands of years wouldn't things get a bit crowded? Now let's reflect on the fact that God did design this world for such a thing in the beginning, before Adam and Eve disobeyed God, in the Garden of Eden. Man sinned and corrupted things on earth, therefore our days are numbered, we have illness and death from old age. Emily, I know it's hard to understand death, but we can't all live forever on earth, at least not until God has accomplished His plans."

"He has plans?"

"Yes, there are plans to create a new earth, where our King Jesus will reign. It will be fashioned, in such a way, that we live eternity with Him. The Believers that are here at that time and all the saints from heaven will live together. Let's read some of that from Revelation 21:1-5 (NIV)."

She grabbed her Bible and turned to the verses she was looking for.

"'Then I saw 'a new heaven and a new earth,' for the first heaven and the first earth had passed away, and there was no longer any sea. I saw the Holy City, the new Jerusalem, coming down out of heaven from God, prepared as a bride beautifully dressed for her husband. And I heard a loud voice from the throne saying, 'Look! God's dwelling place is now among the people, and he will dwell with them. They will be his people, and God himself will be with them and be their God. 'He will wipe every tear from their eyes. There will be no more death' or mourning or crying or pain, for the old order of things has passed away.' He who was seated on the throne said, 'I am making everything new!' Then he said, 'Write this down, for these words are trustworthy and true.'

And if we keep going through verses 22-27, 'I did not see a temple in the city, because the Lord God Almighty and the Lamb are its temple. The city does not need the sun or the moon to shine on it, for the glory of God gives it light, and the Lamb is its lamp. The nations will walk by its light, and the kings of the earth will bring their splendor into it. On no day will its gates ever be shut, for there will be no night there, The glory and honor of the nations will be brought into it. Nothing impure will ever enter it, nor will anyone who does what is shameful or deceitful, but only those whose names are written in the Lamb's book of life* (Revelation 21:22-27 NIV).'"

"Is my name written in that book?" June asked.

"Yes, all our names are written there. We all accepted Jesus, as our Savior."

It had been a long day, wiping a lot of tears away. Answering a lot of difficult questions and the First Lady had not had a break. She did however take the time to ask some of the staff to assist in the funeral arrangements, to take those pressures off her so she could focus on the children and their needs.

The girls were tucked into bed early. It had been a hard, emotional day for all of them.

Before falling off to sleep they collectively said their prayers. The twins were thankful for their new big bed with a canopy, they were all thankful for family, and thankful that George was going to be with Jesus.

"I'm thankful that we can pray together. Our words are strengthened when they are lifted up together. Leviticus 26 tells us how God multiplies our request when we unite. You can read about that tomorrow. It's time for bed." Their mother kissed each child and tucked the twins in to bed.

While Emily made her way to her own room where she added some additional prayers before crawling into bed. Where she thanked God for giving her two dads here, and for Him being her Father in heaven. George had been able to help her get over her fear of being in her own room again, and she was thankful for that as well. The list was long of things she was grateful for, but she heard her mother's voice call down the hall, "lights out."

Jim approached his wife and spoke of how he knew it was hard for Emily to find her biological father, only to lose him after a few months, his heart was breaking for her. She pointed out that God brought them together and allowed George to find Jesus in the process. Reminding him that's it's important to focus on the good things.

"We don't know all the purposes that were intended for our encounter with George, but we do know that George helped us in a difficult time, and we were there for him during his passing."

She pulled out her Bible and turned to Isaiah 55:8-11 (AMP) and read.

"'*For My thoughts are not your thoughts, neither are your ways My ways, says the Lord. For as the heavens are higher than the earth, so are My ways higher than your ways and My thoughts than your thoughts. For as the rain and snow come*

CHAPTER SIXTEEN

down from the heavens, and return not there again, but water the earth and make it bring forth and sprout, that it may give seed to the sower and bread to the eater. So shall My word be that goes forth out of My mouth: it shall not return to Me void [without producing any effect, useless], but it shall accomplish that which I please and purpose, and it shall prosper in the thing for which I sent it.'"

His response, "His ways are higher than ours. I think another purpose for all this was for Emily. She needed to know where she came from, who her people are."

"Her people." That phrase bounced around in her head while remembering the stories that George shared about his upbringing, and how he didn't want that for Emily. They weren't there for him during any of his life's challenges, and they would not have been there for him at his end.

Then she brought up to her husband about the letter George had given her months ago. How he didn't want her to reach out to them until Emily was older. But she was questioning whether she should notify them of his passing. Their addresses were in the letter. What if they want to attend the funeral? But then, what if they wanted to try and manipulate Emily? So many questions, yet she was too tired to focus on any of them.

Jim stated, "I believe that one person can change the direction of the generation to follow. George was trying to change, and I think God will reward him for that. Emily will succeed in making a difference in that family line, without them. A new legacy of blessings will start with her. She has demonstrated many gifts from God already, who will build on her strengths. Can you imagine what else is in store for her?"

Emily felt a cool breeze brush across her face, she turned and saw Rex standing beside her bed. She sat up quickly, knowing that he had come to give her a message to deliver. Rex explained the message was for her this time. God had overseen their sorrow and wanted to deliver a message that would bring them peace. He explained that George was greeted with a great celebration, and he was reunited with his wife, your mother who had gone before him. Jesus himself, showed George his new home, that he had designed just for him.

Rex described his ranch that went on for as far as one could see, with all the cows and horses he could desire. And in his home was his prize possession, the hat that she had given him, and on one of the walls was a mural of the exact painting that April had created. George was happy and wanted her to be happy.

Further explaining that God had rewarded George with many gifts in heaven, for the good that he had done on earth. His sins were forgiven and forgotten. *"For as high as the heavens are above the earth, so great is his love for those who fear him; as far as the east is from the west, so far has he removed our transgressions from us* (Psalm 103:11,12 NIV)." Clarifying that God only looks on the good that was sown. After repentance and acceptance of Jesus as his Savior all is forgiven. Rex shared with Emily that there had been many good deeds of kindness and assistance that George had performed before and while he was incarcerated, that had not gone unnoticed by God. Just because a person makes mistakes in life, doesn't mean that they haven't done good and generous acts. Pointing out that all Scripture is true and is there for one's edification. He gave 1 Timothy 6:17-19 (NIV) as an example to help her understand.

"'Command those who are rich in this present world not to be arrogant nor to put their hope in wealth, which is so uncertain, but to put their hope in God, who richly provides us with everything for our enjoyment. Command them to do good, to be rich in good deed, and to be generous and willing to share. In this way they will lay up treasure for themselves as a firm foundation for the coming age, so that they may take hold of the life that is truly life.'"

Emily was so pleased to hear these words of encouragement and comfort. She thanked Rex and asked him if he was there when George crossed over to heaven. Rex had answered that he had stayed with her, but he knew that there were many present at his passing, and they escorted him home to a huge celebration.

She smiled, because she had seen them all in his room the night of their celebration party. She had thought they had come to celebrate with them. Rex assured her that they had come to celebrate his homecoming.

There was a pause and then Rex stated he had another message, that she was to deliver to her mom. Emily sat up with great anticipation, she had not ever received a message specifically for her mom before.

Rex continued with the message. "She is to receive a gift soon, from Elohim. Have her read Genesis 21 and Luke 1:24." And then he was gone.

Emily was so excited that she couldn't go back to sleep. It was too difficult to wait until morning, she had to share what she had heard. She ran down the hall, banging on the twin's door, then darted off to her parents' room.

Before the twins could rustle up, Emily was in her parent's bed, jumping up and down. The twins came running behind her with wide eyes, curious as to what was going on. They could see how excited Emily was and that rubbed off onto them.

"I just spoke to my angel. He had a message for me. But it's really for all of us."

She began to share everything he had said about George, how he made it home, and how he has a big, beautiful ranch. Adding that there was a huge celebration in heaven for him. She was waving her hands in demonstration of how large it was.

She turned to April with big eyes. "And your mural is on his wall in heaven." And she smiled with such pleasure while saying, "And he has his cowboy hat too."

The whole family was laughing and hugging each other. This was surely good news to share, even in the middle of the night. Then Emily turned to her mom and announced she had a message for her. The First Lady was shocked, she had not ever received a report from Emily before, her heart fluttered with excitement.

She shrugged her shoulders and leaned into Emily with a whisper. "You have a word for me?"

"Yes, that you are going to receive a gift, soon." Stating it matter-of-factly because she had no idea what it meant.

Oh course, she was thinking Jim must have bought her something. But the thought crossed her mind, why would an angel deliver a message like that? She smiled and thanked Emily for delivering the good news to everyone. Recognizing the late hour and that it was time to settle down, mom was the one to break up the party and insisted they all go back to bed. As Emily was leaving the room, she turned to finish delivering the message from her angel.

"I'm sorry, I was so excited I forgot to tell you the rest of the message." She stated apologetically.

"There's more?" Mom seemed confused, although interested.

"Well, he used the name Elohim. Said the gift would be from Him, and that you are to read Genesis 21 and Luke 1:24. What's in those verses, Mom?"

"I'll have to find out and report to you tomorrow morning. For now, good night." Pointing to the door. "Emily, thank you."

Jim looked at his wife. "Elohim means strong Creator God. It communicates both His sovereignty and His authority." He paused, then said. "His ability to accomplish anything."

"Well, I'm not going to get any sleep now. I have got to look up those verses. What kind of gift? Gift of teaching? That would align with our recent conversations. You know that I desire to be a good teacher to my children."

As she was talking, Jim was searching the Scripture. "Um, you might be surprised, as to what it says."

"What? Go ahead read it." Breathlessly awaiting.

"I think you will get the gist in the first three verses of Genesis 21. '*And the LORD visited Sarah as He had said, and the LORD did for Sarah as He had spoken. For Sarah conceived and bore Abraham a son in his old age, at the set time of which God had spoken to him. And Abraham called the name of his son who was born to him—whom Sarah bore to him—Isaac* (Genesis 21:1-3, NKJV).'"

She looked as white as a ghost. Confused, not knowing if she should be scared to death or happy. They had tried for years to conceive a child. It just wasn't in the cards for them. Their busy lifestyle kept them stressed and overworked, but they had always made time for each other, and had tried many times to conceive. They had resided with the idea, that God had wanted them to adopt, so that was the course they had taken. And they have three beautiful, talented girls. This information was hard to comprehend.

"Best read that other scripture to confirm what you and I are thinking."

"That I'm too old to have a child?" She was still in shock, pondering what that could mean.

He turned to Luke 1:24,25 (NKJV). "'*Now after those days his wife Elizabeth conceived; and she hid herself five months, saying, 'Thus the Lord has dealt with me, in the days when He looked on me, to take away my reproach among people.*'"

"Can't get any clearer than that." She stared off into space, wondering if all this could be possible. Yet remembering anything is possible with God.

After snuggling up next to her husband for comfort, trying to hold back any unbelief, it was clear she wasn't going to get any sleep. She got dressed and went downstairs to the kitchen. After a cup of coffee, excitement set in. She decided she was going to prepare a feast to celebrate the good news. When the kitchen staff arrived, they noticed she had things under control, and was having so much fun, preparing every breakfast item she could think of.

She had everyone's favorite and more. She sent the staff away; she wanted it to be a special family time together.

Her husband was the first to arrive for coffee and smelled the delicacies all the way down the hall. "I see you found some energy to cook. A feast no less."

"We have good news to share with the girls and I wanted to make it special."

"What did you do with the kitchen staff?"

"I sent them on a long break." She smiled big.

He came around and grabbed her by the waist and smiled. "You're happy then?"

"Oh yes, very happy." They embraced and were interrupted by giggling girls.

They shared the good news from Emily's angel with the girls. Joyous cheers broke out everywhere. Of course, they had not confirmed anything, nor were they given a time frame, but they believed, and had faith that what God promised would come to pass. They shared Scripture that helped the girls understand along with a lesson on how they were to rely on God. The importance of trust and how we are to believe.

Jim started with Isaiah 55:11 (NASB). "'*So will My word be which goes forth from My mouth; It will not return to Me empty, Without accomplishing what I desire, And without succeeding in the matter for which I sent it.*'"

Mom followed up with Joshua 23:14 (NKJV). "'*Behold, this day I am going the way of all the earth. And you know in all your hearts and in all your souls that not one thing has failed of all the good things which the LORD your God spoke concerning you. All have come to pass for you; not one word of them has failed.*'"

All three girls shouted, "We believe. We believe we are going to have a baby."

They jumped around the kitchen squealing with such joy that the President and First Lady joined in the procession of dancing around the counter and table. The Secret Service showed up to see what the shouting was all about. They observed a family celebrating together, dancing with joy and laughter, and grazing the tremendous spread on the kitchen island. When they were noticed, the First Lady flagged them in and told them there was plenty to go around. They were unaware of what they were so happy about, considering they just lost a friend, but the food looked good, and they couldn't pass up the First Lady's cooking.

The First Lady met with her doctor that same day. There was too much excitement in the air to delay finding out if there was any chance that she would be able to conceive and carry a child. She trusted what God said, but she wanted to confirm with the medical profession. Was there a procedure she needed to follow up with to allow her to conceive? Money was no object, but apparently time may be a factor, considering her age.

To her extraordinary surprise, there was no procedure necessary. Her miracle had already been performed; she was already pregnant. The best the doctor could predict was that she was about five months along. In her mind, that aligned with Scripture, and made sense why the angel gave her two verses, to confirm God's gift.

The doctor proceeded to ask questions, whether there had been any signs that she noticed? How did she not know she was pregnant? She explained that she had been so stressed over the events of the past months, that any signs went unnoticed. Not to mention, the fact pregnancy never occurred to her, considering the years of trying with no success, and her age. The doctor was assuring her that age would not be a factor, many women carry babies late in life and she would have the best of care.

The First Lady didn't share with the doctor that she wasn't actually worried about carrying the child. If God ordained it, she knew everything would be just fine. She was just surprised she was already pregnant, and five months along. Might be why she felt a bit heavier lately. She just thought it was from stress eating and doing less exercise. But apparently, she wasn't going to show much of a belly. Which most women would love, but she was so excited to be with child she wanted to show off a big belly to the world.

The doctor asked if she was wanting an ultrasound done to determine the gender. She was feeling overly excited now, she was glowing, and it was more than just from being pregnant. It was God's glory that she was feeling. The fact she found out God was giving her such a wonderful gift, then to find out she was already pregnant, and now she can know the gender. Had she realized all this was going on in one day, she would have brought Jim with her. She was reminded that God only needs a day, to accomplish what He desires. He speaks things into existence. How we serve a wonderful God. She burst into Scripture reciting Isaiah 12:2-6 (NIV). As if everyone did that when they found out good news.

"'Behold, God is my salvation, I will trust and not be afraid; For the LORD GOD is my strength and song, And He has become my salvation.' Therefore you will joyously draw water from the springs of salvation. And in that day you will say, 'Give thanks to the LORD, call on His name. Make known His deeds among the peoples; Make them remember that His name is exalted.' Praise the LORD in song, for He has done excellent things; Let this be known throughout the earth. Cry aloud and shout for joy.'"

Her enthusiasm and joy rubbed off on all those in the office. It was a wonderful opportunity, to share the goodness of God and His name, Elohim. His ability to accomplish anything, even gifting a barren woman with child. Sharing Psalm 109:27 (NIV) with any and everybody that would listen.

"'Let them know that it is your hand, that you, LORD have done it.'"

On her way back home to the mansion she was trying to think of a creative way to share the good news with the family. How were they going to start this miraculous journey together.

CHAPTER SIXTEEN

It was decided to keep the good news quiet until dessert. A special cake had been purchased that would reveal the gender, along with the fact that she was for sure pregnant. It was not something they would have to wait long for.

God had continually rewarded them with joyous celebrations. He had turned their mourning to joy in revealing this good news.

Song "Everything" by Lauren Daigle

Chapter Seventeen

Time of Rejoicing

The staff assisted the First Lady with all the arrangements for the funeral services. It was to be a simple gathering of the First Family, a few friends, along with the house staff and agents that guard the family, that had all gotten to know George from working at the house. The President had carried out his plans to share the Gospel with his household and they had been receptive to his messaging, which pleased them all. It had lifted everyone's spirits to know that they were working for a godly man that went so far as to minister to them.

The President was to deliver the eulogy, April's artwork was stretched into a frame and was to be displayed, and June was to play the piece she had composed for George's celebration. Everyone was wanting to do something special for the event. Not only had the family come to love George, but those around him had come to appreciate him, they saw him as an overcomer, and recognized all that he had done for the family in their time of need. In their eyes he was a hero.

The guests were greeted with smiles, comments were shared among them of little jokes and stories that George had shared. It was a joyous occasion. The President took to the podium and began to share that he was thankful for the opportunity to get to know this man, that they had come to honor.

"'God works in mysterious ways,' seems to be a cliche, but it's been our reality. You have all shared stories about how George touched your lives. Yet, George would tell you, how all of you shaped his last days."

People were looking on listening yet visualizing the small ways they had come to know George.

"We came to know this man with a checkered past, who tried to break in our home, witnessed a crime committed against our family, assisted us in escaping what could have been death for us, only to become our trusted bodyguard and friend. One who made sure we were provided for and cared for. God took an unlikely candidate and made him our hero. God restored this man's dignity and honor, but most importantly he welcomed him into His family, and we welcomed him into ours."

Tears were welling up in the girl's eyes as their father continued. "George came to know Christ Jesus as his Savior, through an opportunity given to us to share the Gospel with him. Just as we have recently done with many of you. No one knows when they will take their last breath, if you have not accepted Jesus Christ as your Savior and Lord, then I beseech you to come to know Him as the Son of God. Don't delay, repent, and ask Him for forgiveness. He will forgive, and all will be forgotten. You can start this day with a clean slate. We are all given second chances and new beginnings, with the Lord. He will embrace you and bless you.

There is a place that He prepares for you in heaven, where there is no more sadness, strife, or worrying, there is no more illness or death. We are promised that treasures are laid up in heaven for us. Psalm 37:4 (NKJV) *'Delight yourself also in the LORD, And He shall give you the desires of your heart.'* We've heard that George made it home, and he has a ranch in heaven, which he desired, and is surrounded by many familiar gifts from the girls. How he treasured and loved the girls. Gifts and rewards from God, that are given from acts of generosity, kindness, and goodness are treasured. Yet, the greatest gift of all, is knowing that Jesus loves you. Your desires can be fulfilled in heaven, but you must first get there. The only way is Jesus."

He looked out at the faces before him and smiled, while stating the obvious about himself. "Never miss an opportunity to share the Gospel of Jesus with someone."

His wife smiled back at him, and it encouraged him to go on.

"I stand here before you, knowing that what is in the Word, is true. We have seen God's Word fulfilled in our lives, and I know that it can be so for you as well. I am reminded of a poem, we read as a family the other day. It talks of how people perceive Christians, I'm standing before you, as one that needs Jesus in my life. I need His cleansing as much as the next man. God reminds me that I can lean on Him, and that I am worthy of His love and grace. He offers that to you as well."

He stopped to let that comment sink-in to those listening. He knew that this was an opportunity to witness and bring others to Christ, and he didn't want to rush through it. He wanted them to grasp what he was saying. He continued, after looking around the room and making specific eye contact, with some of those present, that needed to hear the message. His first attempts with some of them may not have gone the way he had hoped, but he wasn't giving up.

What he may say next could have consequences for the family, but the company that was being kept today could be trusted.

"We recognized that God was able to use the least of these among us. God used George, He used a child to deliver messages that saved all our lives, which we are grateful for. Jesus used His Word in the Bible to communicate with us, the Holy Spirit guided us in wisdom and truths. We are here today, because of those truths and the fact that we listened. Your help is there if you seek it, listen for it, obey it, and follow it into deliverance. George didn't miss his opportunity. This is a time of rejoicing; we are celebrating George's homecoming."

He went on to share more good news, that they would be welcoming a new addition to the family, in about four months. They were told to prepare for a house full of joy. Timely congratulations and celebrations broke out throughout the room.

Emily sat on the front row beaming with joy, through the entire service. She not only appreciated the people who came to share this moment with them, but she saw the room filled with angels. Rex was standing at the front, smiling, with his eyes on Emily. He was letting her know, that heaven was watching from above and celebrating with all of them as well.

Song "Who You Are To Me" by Chris Tomlin, ft. Lady

Chapter Eighteen

Reflection

The President and First Lady reflected on the Words that had been delivered over these events and were able to see how precise God's messaging had been for them. How they had found courage and strength needed to get them through difficult times. They stayed steadfast in His Word and found peace and assurances, that all would be well. They even received blessings from God through the messages shared. Their journey continues on with the assignment that God has given them.

Proverbs 3:13, Taught them to gain understanding through the Word.

Proverbs 3:21, Where they were told to use discretion and find wisdom.

Proverbs 3:26, Reminded them that the Lord will be their confidence and security.

John 14:15, Had them focus on the fact that help dwells within them.

Proverbs 3:31-38, Assured them God would deal with evil agendas.

Luke 21, Warned of betrayals.

John 16:5-14, Showed truth and righteousness prevails and the sinful are judged.

Proverbs 4:20, Stressed that life was found in the Word.

Proverbs 4:23, Life springs forth from the heart.

Luke 1:24, The news that she conceived was a gift from God.

Proverb 28:18,28 (NIV) *"The one whose walk is blameless is kept safe, but the one whose ways are perverse will fall into the pit. When the wicked rise to power, people go into hiding; but when the wicked perish, the righteous thrive."*

It was clear to them that they only needed to reflect on Jesus who dwells within. He speaks in a still small voice that can be heard when you are listening for it and focusing on Jesus. Spending time in His Word will allow for clarity of His message to pop from the pages, and the Holy Spirit will be given the opportunity to lead in truth.

"Take delight in the Lord, and He will give your hearts desires" Psalm 37:4 (NLT).

Song "God Is In This Story" by Katy Nichole, Big Daddy Weave

About the Author

Author, **Jayda Lee Wilson**, will admit that formulating words into a written work was not her forte, until she partnered with the Holy Spirit. Now embracing the move of the Holy Spirit in her life, she finds pleasure conveying the Lord's messages through stories. The task presented to her was to encourage others to seek a closer relationship with the Lord, through books of fiction. She recognized that God has a different purpose for our lives in each season of life. There was a time that she and her husband would not have thought they would be teachers, but stepping forward in faith, they became dedicated teachers in the Children's wing for twenty years. Participating in years of Women's Bible Studies and leading a small women's group in studies prepared her for a short season of writing devotions. Then the Holy Spirit guided her into yet another season, to author books. We are all a work in progress to fulfill a purpose that God has on our lives. Her season of life as an Interior Designer allowed her creativity to flow and now, she uses it to touch other's lives. God has now used her creativity to progress as a published author, to tell the stories that God wants shared. Her first published work was "The Jump", later released was the sequel where the Exodus continued from the Dome in "Return To The City". Inspiration continued to flow and "Life Choices, Assignment From God" was written and published and there are many more books to follow. It's a delight to share stories that overflow with God's truths and His written Word for others to enjoy. Outside of writing she has a heart to volunteer when needed and is committed to serve the Lord in whatever way He leads.

End Notes

Bible Sources:

New King James Version (NKJV): Scripture taken from the NEW KING JAMES VERSION, Copyright © 1982 by Thomas Nelson, Inc.

King James Version (KJV): Public Domain

The Passion Translation (TPT): Copyright © 2017, 2018, 2020 by Passion & Fire Ministries, Inc.

New American Standard Bible (NASB): Scripture taken from NEW AMERICAN STANDARD BIBLE, Copyright © 2020 By The Lockman Foundation

New International Version (NIV): Scripture taken from the HOLY BIBLE, NEW INTERNATIONAL VERSION, Copyright ©1973,1978,1984,2011 by Biblica, Inc.

Amplified Bible (AMP): Scripture taken from the AMPLIFIED BIBLE, Copyright ©2015 by the Lockman Foundation

New Living Translation (NLT): Scriptures taken from the HOLY BIBLE, NEW LIVING TRANSLATION, Copyright ©1996,2004,2007,2015 by Tyndale House Foundation

The Living Bible (TLB): Scriptures taken from the LIVING BIBLE Copyright© 1971 by Tyndale House Foundation

New Century Version (NCV): Scriptures taken from The Everyday Bible, New Century Version, Copyright © 2005 by Thomas Nelson Inc.

Chapter One

Proverbs 3:13   NKJV
Proverbs 3:21-26   NKJV
Proverbs 3:31-35   NKJV
Song "Keep Me In The Moment" by Jeremy Camp

Chapter Two

Proverbs 3:13   NKJV
Proverbs 3:22   NKJV
Proverbs 4:20-23   NKJV
Proverbs 4:5   NKJV
Luke 15:5,6   NKJV
Song "Always" by Chris Tomlin

Chapter Three

| Proverbs 3:26 | NASB |

Song "Raise A Hallelujah" by Jonathan Helser

Chapter Four

Galatians 6:9	NKJV
Joshua 1:8,9	NCV
Psalm 91:11,12	NASB
Matthew 18:10	NASB
Isaiah 41:10	NCV

Song "Hold On To Me" by Lauren Daigle

Chapter Five

Luke 21:15-19	NKJV
Psalm 50:6	NKJV
Psalm 50:1-7	NKJV
Psalm 50:12,14,15	NKJV
Psalm 50:16-23	NKJV
Isaiah 33:22	NKJV
Job 12:22,23	NKJV
Psalm 102:27,28	NKJV

Song "Yes He Can" by CAIN

Chapter Six

Proverbs 4:22	NKJV
Proverbs 4:23	NKJV
Proverbs 3:24	NKJV
Luke 21:4	NKJV

| Matthew 16:24-27 | NKJV |
| Luke 21:15 | NKJV |

Chapter Seven

| Job 12:4-6 | AMP |
| Job 12:9-12 | AMP |

Chapter Eight

| Romans 8:31-39 | NIV |
| Matthew 13:41,42 | NKJV |

Chapter Nine

Revelation 21:5-8	AMP
Psalm 139:5	TPT
Psalm 139:14-16	TPT
Romans 10:17	NIV
Colossians 1:12-14	AMP
1 Peter 3:4	NKJV
Psalm 25:4-11	NASB

Song "I'm Going To Walk With Jesus" by Consumed by Fire

Chapter Ten

Deuteronomy 28:12	NKJV
Psalm 36:8	NIV
Philippians 4:19	NKJV
John 16:23,24	NKJV
Job 22:28	NKJV
1 Samuel 17:36	NKJV

1 Samuel 17:40,42	NKJV
1 Samuel 17:45-47	NKJV
Psalm 35:1-8	NASB

Song "Confidence" by Sanctus Real

Chapter Eleven

Hebrews 13:2	NIV
Colossians 1:16	NASB
Matthew 26:53	NASB

Song "Speak To The Mountains" by Chris McClarney

Chapter Twelve

1 Kings 14:22-24	NKJV
Psalm 77:11,12	NKJV
Matthew 28:18-20	NKJV
Philippians 2:4	NKJV
Philippians 2:13-15	NKJV
Hebrews 12:25-29	NKJV
Hosea 4:6-9	AMP
Proverbs 16:18	NIV84
2 Timothy 3:1-5	NASB
1 Samuel 30:8	NKJV
Psalm 59:1,2	NKJV
Luke 1:37	NKJV
Psalm 7:6-11	NASB
Psalm 7:14-16	NASB
Jeremiah 8:22	NIV
Jeremiah 46:12	NIV

Jeremiah 23:24,26,27,32,39,40	NASB
Luke 21:15	NKJV
Psalm 140:1-3	NKJV
Psalm 27:1-3	NKJV
Proverbs 3:35	NKJV
Isaiah 41:9-13	NKJV
Quote:	Martin Luther King Jr.

https://www.brainyquote.com/quotes/martin_luther_king_jr_10922

Song "Me On Your Mind" by Matthew West

Chapter Thirteen

Job 38:4-7	NKJV
2 Corinthians 6:18	NKJV
1 John 3:1-3	NKJV
1 John 5:1-5	NKJV
Ephesians 1:5-7	NKJV
Luke 6:35	AMP
Luke 6:36,37	AMP
Hebrews 8:12	NIV
Matthew 6:14	NIV
Luke 17:3	NASB
Matthew 5:44-47	AMP

Poem "When I Say I Am A Christian" by Carol Wimmer 1988 https://whenisayiamachristian.com

Quote: Martin Luther King Jr. https://www.brainyquote.com/quotes/martin_luther_king_jr_109228

2 Chronicles 7:14	NKJV

Song "When You Speak" by Jeremy Camp

Chapter Fourteen

Proverbs 29:16	AMP
Luke 19:13	NKJV
John 14:13-21	NIV

Patrick Henry, "The Virginian" April 1956 issue

Isaiah 43:19	NLT
Psalm 33:12	NKJV
Proverbs 3:5-8	NKJV
Joshua 24:15	NIV
Romans 12:17-21	NIV
2 Corinthians 2:14-15	NCV
Matthew 10:32-39	NIV
Acts 16:34	NASB
James 5:15,16	NKJV
Mark 12:31	NKJV
Isaiah 32:18	NKJV

Quotes Thomas Jefferson https://www.azquotes.com/quote/1411168

2 Chronicles 7:14	NKJV

Song "Gifts From God" by Chris Tomlin, ft. Christ Lane

Chapter Fifteen

Psalm 19:1	AMP
Genesis 1:14,16	NKJV

Book Reference The Real Meaning of the Zodiac by Dr. James Kennedy, Ph.D.

John 17:14	NASB
John 17:22,23	NASB

Proverbs 17:22
Proverbs 16:24 NIV
John 14:2,3 NASB
Isaiah 32:18 NIV
Proverbs 24:3 NIV
Billy Graham https://www.brainyquote.com/quotes/billy_graham_382921
1 Corinthians 13:12 TLB
Revelation 22:5 NIV
Psalm 34:20-22 NKJV
Psalm 100:1-5 NKJV
Song "My Jesus" by Anne Wilson

Chapter Sixteen

139:1-6, 13-18 NASB
Revelation 21:1-5 NIV
Revelation 21:22-27 NIV
Isaiah 55:8-11 AMP
Psalm 103:11,12 NIV
1 Timothy 6:17-19 NIV
Genesis 21:1-3 NKJV
Luke 1:24,25 NKJV
Isaiah 55:11 NASB
Joshua 23:14 NKJV
Isaiah 12:2-6 NIV
Psalm 109:27 NIV
Song "Everything" by Lauren Daigle

Chapter Seventeen

Psalm 37:4   NKJV

Song "Who You Are To Me" by Chris Tomlin, ft Lady

Chapter Eighteen

Proverbs 28:18,28   NIV

Psalm 27:4   NLT

Song "God Is In This Story" by Katy Nichole, Big Daddy Weave

Summary

Romans 8:28   NKJV